Diversion Books
A Division of Diversion Publishing Corp.
443 Park Avenue South, Suite 1008
New York, New York 10016
www.DiversionBooks.com

For more information, email info@diversionbooks.com

First Diversion Books edition July 2015.
Print ISBN: 978-1-62681-636-7
eBook ISBN: 978-1-62681-635-0

JONESBRIDGE

ECHOES OF HINTERLAND

M.E. PARKER

DIVERSIONBOOKS

With special thanks to Elizabeth Kracht, whose insight and tireless devotion was the beacon that guided *Jonesbridge* through the smoke. The literary landscape is a brighter place with her in it, and I am grateful that she couldn't have imagined a world without *Jonesbridge*. And to the talented and lovely Kate Parker, wife and reader, without whom the inspiration would wane.

"In Soft Regions, Soft Men are born."

—HERODOTUS

CHAPTER 1

As Myron's arms and legs adjusted to the pull, the clock struck again. Pain shot through his limbs when the gears, one at each corner of the table, advanced another notch, threatening to tear him apart.

An unseen projector parted the darkness with a beam of light. Flickering to life on a screen above him, a grainy film entitled *A New Day in Jonesbridge* began with a panoramic sunrise over mountains and a bugle corps sounding the anthem of the Alliance. "Welcome to the Jonesbridge Industrial Complex, the jewel of the Continental Alliance," a pleasant female narrator stated. The reel skipped, filling the screen with lines, interrupting her statement, and resumed with sweeping views of the factories, mines, and Industry workers, *slogs* she called them, performing their duties with purpose in the "New Jonesbridge" under the glow of morning sun.

Myron tugged at the chains shackled to his wrists and

ankles, hoping for a moment of relief, but his restraints had him locked down in spread eagle, his bones popping in rhythm with each tick of the stretcher clock behind him.

The film continued with two slogs loading a cannon barrel onto a barge. The artillery assembly plant shimmered beneath a clear blue sky behind them. "The survival of our Alliance and our way of life depends on the secret location of this facility and its capability. Black market privateers and traitors who aid the enemy are always at the ready when loose tongues spill information." The scene showed two men in orange jumpsuits apprehending a woman whispering into another woman's ear. "Travel to and from Jonesbridge is restricted to train operators, who are dedicated members of the Defense Administration." A man in a gray smock saluted two men on a train platform. "Leaving the complex is therefore prohibited and *unnecessary* until the grand conclusion of the war. As a wise man once observed, three can keep a secret if two of them are dead."

Myron tried to wiggle his toes and discovered he had lost feeling in his extremities. He wished the same would happen to the rest of his body, but he ached and throbbed as though his bones might break right through his skin.

"...Jonesbridge is a *safe* place bound by the protective Great Gorge. Spanning more than 2,850 feet and plummeting to depths of 700 feet, where the outflow of victory production waste flows, the Great Gorge is deep enough to keep the E'sters at bay and wide enough to thwart their artillery should they ever find us." A curtain of smoke masked the other side of a smoldering fissure in the earth, dissolving into scenes of busy workers dismantling a wrecked war wagon.

"Recent success in battle has given our intrepid mobile salvage squads new territory to scour for usable materials. What this means is more rewarding work and less idle time for everyone here at Jonesbridge. No matter what your contribution, be it a *machinist*," the film showed a man holding a set of calipers to a part in mid-formation on the lathe. "*Assembler*," the pictures continued with a close-up of a woman fitting an armored fender over the wheel of an overloader. The list went on, zooming in on factory slogs performing duties expeditiously. "*Miner, forger, cleaner, maintenance, riveter, tool and die, salvager,* each of you is an invaluable gear in our industrial machine."

Myron's tongue sat in his mouth like a piece of shoe leather. He tried to siphon sweat droplets from his upper lip to quench his thirst, but even his perspiration had dried in the chill of the brick chamber.

Images of fields replaced the factories. "Our uncontaminated farmlands continue to dwindle and must now produce more food per acre than ever before to supply soldiers with the nutrients needed to wage battle. In Jonesbridge, slogs have learned the value of food through many years of wartime scarcity." Footage of slogs enjoying their daily rations in the commons filled the screen. Myron's anticipation of a meal like that one gave him the drive to endure his pain.

He rocked his head, the only body part he could still move, as the film resumed with more images of the mines and factories, all hands satisfied and working hard. "Everyone at Jonesbridge pulls his weight. You will be paid for your efforts piecemeal. The more you do, the easier it will be to afford your daily rations and your domicile. While you are here, you will have nothing to worry about except the duties the Industry Administration requires you to perform. Loyal, patriotic, hardworking citizens in the Industry Administration will be rewarded for their sacrifices when we emerge victorious—when we finally secure enough uncontaminated farmland to feed our people."

When the narrator's voice faded and the screen went black Myron hoped his agony would end soon. He waited for release, for the tension in his limbs to subside, but instead of a reprieve, the projector resumed its vibrato hum. The triumphant call of bugles gave way to pounding drums and a chorus of voices shouting and crying, pleading for mercy. Flames danced on the screen, reflecting red up the walls of the brick chamber. Black smoke and ash fell from the sky in the film, blackening the sun.

Myron jerked his hips up, hoping to relieve the tension on his legs while images of wreckage and explosions filled the screen—maimed and weeping people, dead men and women piled up in a hill. Watching the carnage, enduring the tug of his bones, Myron feared he would share the same death as the soldiers in the film, disembodied and broken.

The narrator's diction transformed into a harsh staccato scolding. "*This* is what happens when our countrymen don't have the proper equipment for battle. *This*," she said, flashing another gruesome picture, "is what happens to your countrymen when *you* don't do your job." A collage of dead and burning farmland persisted on the screen. "That agonizing stretch you are now experiencing is the way everyone feels when *you* shirk your duty. With ten people to feed and only one piece of bread, ten fireboxes to fuel and only one piece of coal, ten filthy E'ster soldiers to shoot with only one bullet. We are all called upon to make sacrifices in our troubling age. Take pride in your work. Take pride in your shift mates. Take pride in the Alliance. So that they take pride in you."

Myron's stomach wrenched and then he wet himself, relief and dread in the same instant. Lying in his own fluids, the clock struck again. The chains moved. Myron screamed. The film began anew.

He tried to count his way through a playing of the film, agonizing over how many times this would happen, how many ticks of the clock, how many pulls of the chains until his arms and legs slipped right out of their joints, yanking his flesh right along with them. He didn't know how long he could endure the narrator, a voice that sounded so much like his mother who had died when Myron was only six.

The air in his lungs thinned as the stretching continued. He sipped breaths, one at a time, to quench his thirst for oxygen, certain he would die on this table. In his seventeen years, Myron had broken both an arm and a leg, cut his stomach on a wire fence, and been struck on the head by an errant steam piston, but never had he felt his life leaving his body—the way his mother's had—all for the *protection of future generations.*

His heart slowed, thumping harder, pushing air to his numbing fingers and toes as his head spun. If he were to croak at this very moment, he longed to see his mother's face. He tried to summon her, but all that appeared was the horrible picture of the last time he saw her with the vegetable hatchet lodged in her forehead. Everything went dark. He struggled to hang on, but only the ticking of the stretcher clock tethered him to the world.

When the door swung open, new sounds filtered in.

Myron felt a sting on his face, a slap. The tension on his limbs released. He moaned, sucking in a deep breath. A bright light switched on. Two guards' faces floated in and out of the spectral light above him, making them look like spirits, their voices intertwined with the sounds of tugging chains. The *ghosts* lifted Myron up and put a skin of water to his lips and handed him a burlap sack with two protein sticks no wider than his finger and a hunk of bread.

His arms hung motionless from dislocated shoulders. His knees buckled, and his ankles gave way as they dragged him through the door and up toward a gray sky, the ache in his joints overpowering the relief of no longer being stretched. On the stairs he passed two orange shirts, two ghosts, escorting another slog down to the stretcher block. A choking cloud of sulfur greeted them as they emerged into daylight. Flanked by his escorts, Myron stumbled down a roadway where countless chimney stacks towered in the mountains' shadows like soot-blackened gatekeepers holding the sun at bay.

They stopped in front of a rotund building with arched doorways encircling it. A single wall, lined on both sides by smock hooks, divided the building in half, one side for men, the other side for women. The guards shoved Myron to the ground and waited under one of the archways, leaving him with no idea of what to do next. He observed large tubs filled with dozens of his fellow slogs, naked, waist-deep in sand, rubbing the grains on their skin, using the abrasion of the sand to clean their skin instead of wasting fresh water.

"What do I do?" Myron whispered.

In the nearest basin, a much older man motioned to Myron, averting his eyes from the ghosts at the door. "Bath."

He gestured by running his hands up his torso and over his head. "Take it off."

Myron crawled toward the edge of the sand basin and removed his smock, covering his private areas with his hands. The man waved him into the basin. "First, coarse grains. Then move to the fine grains." He pointed to another set of tubs across the room.

"Where's the water?" Myron asked.

"Boilers and hydro. Clean water's for drinking only."

"Quiet over there!" One of the ghosts under the archway marched to the edge of the basin and smacked the man next to Myron in the ribs with a discipline rod. The man doubled over with a moan.

The warm sand soothed Myron's muscles as he burrowed low into the grains, scooping handfuls over his stomach. He imagined lying on a beach near the ocean, something he longed to see someday. Before the orange shirts took him away, Myron's grandfather had given him a relic from a long ago time, a postcard of a beach paradise in a place called Bora Bora.

A bell tolled. Scores of naked slogs emerged from the sand, heading for their smocks along the wall. Still nearly immobile from the stretcher, Myron crawled for his smock, concealing his privates. A sudden jolt from one of the ghost's rods stole his breath. He fell back, clutching his stomach as he rolled on the ground. "Up."

With the aid of the guards, Myron trudged through an archway down a narrow corridor, head down, trying to muster enough energy to keep from collapsing. They stopped at a jagged opening, greeted by a wall of hot air. After a jab from a rod, Myron stepped through the hole into a circular chamber with a bed of coals glowing under a chimney vent.

They helped him into the farther of two antique chairs, the kind his grandfather called dentist seats, and strapped his hands, palms down, on the armrests and secured his legs to the base. "*Industry*, Martino," the ghost hollered to a geezer stoking the coal fire.

The old man turned around and opened a drawer next to the chair. "Open up."

He tapped Myron's cheek to open his mouth. Martino shoved a wad of dried leaves under Myron's tongue. "Billet thistle. For pain."

After that, he placed a strip of leather in Myron's mouth. "Bite down." Martino, close to seventy, kept his head down. He showed Myron the back of his own hand, the wrinkly mark of a hammer, gear, and wheel.

The billet thistle reminded Myron of a grassy version of his mom's turnip soup, but the leather tasted like dirt, sweat, and the drool of a thousand people who had sat there before him. He tried hard not to vomit at the taste and then the stink of his own burning flesh. When the red hot branding iron seared the image of a hammer over a gear and axle and Myron's personal identifier on his right hand, he coughed and let out a faint scream.

"Bite down."

After Martino branded Myron's other hand, he wiped them clean of blood and wrapped them with burlap, then pulled the leather strap from Myron's mouth. He returned to the drawer and produced a pair of blunted rusty scissors. As chunks of hair trickled down Myron's back, his mind raced about how he could possibly make it all the way to

Bora Bora now.

Martino glanced up at the two ghosts by the door, never looking them in the eye, and nodded. Each grabbing an elbow, they aided Myron to his feet. The room spun when he stood. With his stomach grumbling, he spat out the billet thistle under his tongue and vomited.

"Quad 14," one of the ghosts said, checking his clipboard, ushering Myron outside. His hands, now bearing the mark of Industry, stung when the icy wind whipped under the burlap wrapping. First left, then a right—they traversed the network of brick roadways that connected domicile quadrangles to factories and delivery depots to coal yards. Against a gray sky, the rows of smokestacks and red bricks blurred together with the hum of turbines as he concentrated on not collapsing, until he was jarred by the sound of a scuffle. A girl, about his age, fought her two escorts as they tried to corral her.

"Where are you taking me?" she screamed, turning to run.

Two other ghosts jogged up to help restrain her. She slung her arms in all directions, keeping her escorts at bay until the biggest ghost of the four smacked her in the back with a discipline rod. She fell to her knees, head down, her hair resembling scattered hay.

Myron rubbed his hands, still covered in burlap to protect the raw branded flesh from the sting of the wind. He saw no such protection on her hands and no Industry tattoos as a ghost on each side grabbed her arms. The girl's eyes grew wild before she bit the ghost's arm so hard her jaw bulged.

"Whores hairpin!" He jumped back, swatting the girl's

face off his arm. "This carpie needs a lesson." The guard rubbed his arm, while the others, now four of them, each took a swat at her with their discipline rods.

"Doc's going to have his hands full sterilizing this one." One of the ghosts tied the girl's hands. They led her away toward the stretcher chamber by a rope, the girl twisting and screaming and kicking up dust. Witnessing her defiance gave Myron hope.

CHAPTER 2

Standing behind his grandfather's house in the twilight of early summer, fireflies wheeled around him, blinking on and off. Mesmerized by their flight, Myron followed their path through the air until one landed on his arm with a sting. Behind that one, other blinks of light, sparks, fluttered through the air, alighting on his workbench where they twinkled into darkness taking his grandfather's house with them. Myron extinguished the cutting torch and hammered flat the points of an iron gear he had just reshaped into the form of a star, which ended up only about half the size of the palm of his hand.

With a dull thud he banged the star a second time, flattening it as much as he could. Then he pinched the tongs around its middle and held it under the overhead lamp to inspect its shape. Mostly star-like he figured, with the exception of the fifth point, which was folded over a bit.

When Myron noticed the starry shadow climbing up

the brick wall by his table, the star having been under his lamp for several seconds, he checked over his shoulder to see if anyone else had seen it. Then he dipped his creation into a bucket where it responded with a hiss, after which he situated the star into a clamp, reached for his awl, and scratched the words *Sindra's Star* across the middle. It wasn't a real engraving, but still something special, though stars of any kind, especially real ones, were a rarity through the blanket of smoke over Jonesbridge.

"What was that?" Rolf, the salvage floor boss, turned on his heel. Myron froze. "Let's have a look." Rolf positioned his magnifying monocle over his good eye, squeezing the other socket shut, and leaned over Myron's workbench. Rolf was a scraggy rope of a man. He was bone-thin, same as the rest of them, but he had more of what passed for muscle than anyone Myron had seen in Jonesbridge, and he stood at least a head taller than any slog on the line—everyone but Myron. Standing eye to eye with Rolf, maybe even a smidge higher, made it difficult for Myron to avert his eyes.

Myron looked away, but *that* showed disrespect. Down, right, then left, and finally his gaze landed on Rolf's head— of all places, Rolf's scalp—a landscape of moles and freckles between paltry tufts of hair. That view gave Myron a grim reminder of what *he* had to look forward to in the near future. He dreaded winding up like everybody else, but, of all the duties in Jonesbridge, Myron was glad they'd assigned him to salvage. It allowed him to follow in the footsteps of his tinkering grandfather who constructed useful contraptions from nothing but junk.

"Just an old gear," Myron said.

"I've never seen a gear like that." Rolf grabbed the tongs

and fished the item out of the bucket, adjusting his monocle to examine the star, now dripping with sanitizing liquid. "Gear, huh?" Rolf said. His magnified eye reminded Myron of the mammoth sea creatures in his grandfather's stories.

"A gear that I changed a little," Myron said. He played dumb, bowing his head, eyes on the floor, an act that had gotten him out of trouble many times.

Rolf held the star to the light. "What's that scribble?" he pointed to the words *Sindra's Star* scrawled into the metal.

"I don't know," Myron said. He was thankful that, like everyone else in Jonesbridge, Rolf couldn't read. Myron scanned the factory for Sindra, who worked on the other side of salvage, wondering if she'd noticed Rolf at Myron's station.

Rolf whipped around to survey the factory floor, eyeing a bank of workers on the other end of the expansive salvage bay. "What—or who—do you keep looking at?" His monocle fell from his eye and snapped back to swing on its leather strap. He stood a bit on his tiptoes, so he could inch up to the same height as Myron before he spoke. "The carpie? Is that who?"

When any man called Sindra a carpie it made Myron want to punch him in the mouth. Sindra had been a rail-walker when the orange shirts caught her, hiking the railroad tracks in search of pockets of civilization. They were orphans, trinket merchants, pickpockets, fortune-tellers, but *not* carpies, who, rumor had it, did nothing but attend to the sexual needs of soldiers.

"Thousands of your *countrymen* are getting blown to smithereens, and you're wasting time with *this*?" Rolf pressed into Myron until their noses touched, until Rolf's breath, heavy with the odor of cinders and salt pork, mixed with his own. "Nobody," he yelled, swatting the workbench with a strip of angle iron, "ever gets out of here with anything other than the bare ass they were born with."

"Yes, sir. I mean, no, sir. Nothing leaves."

"Back to work." Rolf flipped the star over in his hand before pitching it into the steel bin on Myron's bench.

Myron reached for the rope above his head and gave it a tug. A jumble of crumpled metal gears tumbled through a door in the wall. Parts from a hand-crank food processor, he figured, the kind that pulverized bone into meal for the old folks to mix with water and suck through a straw. Myron selected a pair of needle-nose pliers from his tool rack and began the process of extracting tiny steel teeth from the gear, glancing at his iron bin, checking up on the star.

Yanking teeth off chains, toggling, ticking and tocking, wrenching, cutting, splitting one piece of dead machinery after another, Myron bided time until his shift ended. He had only the throb of the turbines and tinkling of metal scraps to mark the seconds off the day. Not resting or eating, or even planning his escape mattered more at the end of his shift than seeing Sindra.

Another yank of the rope and the flap door swung open; this time jewelry and personal accoutrements rolled onto his workbench, things Myron never saw anyone actually wear. And with this batch, a purpling finger that resembled a bloated frankfurter with knuckles, still wearing a bejeweled ring that must have been on too tight to remove in the field. Myron reached for his lime shaker and powdered the finger with lime for the odor, but it still had a smell, a human scent that no amount of lime could absorb.

Myron sucked in a deep breath and positioned his sorting bins in the proper order: rinse, sanitizer, fodder, material. He sandwiched the finger with his tongs and wrangled the pliers around the ring, gold with sapphires that would have shimmered if not for the lime. He dipped the ring into the rinse bin then dropped it into the sanitizer where it fizzled into a turbid green liquid. The finger he tossed into the fodder bucket, picturing the person that once wore that ring. It would have been easy to pass them all off as the faceless enemy, but he often put a face behind the rubble he processed. It made his job more important somehow, more personal than just transferring a digit from one bin to another. He imagined the hand that owned that finger, maybe a woman's hand, a young woman with a mane of black hair spilling down her neck, a mole or two on her cheek and tattoos of beetles and butterflies fluttering up her arms, living alone in a hut on the beach near a harbor full of ancient ships where the rising tide smashed against a coastal fortress of rock. The image of the rest of her body, parts, such as this finger, spread to all quadrants, exploded his dream. So he bid her farewell to rest in peace.

A garbled whistle echoed from the voice box on Myron's table, signaling the end of his shift. He located his buckets and hoisted them one by one to the counter, starting with silver, then copper, steel, tin, and gold. Myron gazed at the green sanitizing liquid bubble across the rack like a waterfall into the river of sludge that churned under the floor.

Aside from his orientation and time in the stretcher block a few months ago, today had been the longest day yet in Jonesbridge, longer than full-clock double-shifts, slower than half-ration detention stints, more painful than losing a toe to the frost last month. Myron shifted his weight. Pain shot through his abdomen. He imagined Sindra, how lovely and wild she was. Then he predicted what this place would certainly do to her given enough time, that it might snuff out her spirit that had inspired him from the first time he saw her when she fought off the guards.

Myron surveyed the line of his fellow piecemeal workers, heads down, eyes on their strainers. Behind him, only the aft wall. Across the aisle, Rolf counted the line foreman's gold. Myron reached behind his back, keeping his smock over his private areas, and relaxed his anus with a sigh—relief, at last. A small red ball, one of his grandfather's fishing antiques, popped out into his hand, something his grandfather had called a bob. It was one of the only things of his grandfather's he had managed to keep, and, as painful as it had been to smuggle in, that bob was Myron's only idea at getting anything out of the factory.

He glanced up again, checking for any eyes that might be on him, and tugged the hem of his smock until he found a loose thread. He jerked the thread and rubbed it along the side of the workbench until the string snapped. Then he threaded it through a hole in the red bob, where fishing line would have once dangled with bait until a fish pulled it under. "Visual confirmation," his grandfather had instructed. "Float goes down and you've hooked one."

On the other end of the string, Myron tied a knot to a loop he had fashioned on the star, the prize Rolf had been so sure would never make it out of the factory that he left it in Myron's iron bin. He flipped over the star and ran his finger across the scratched letters. Then he checked again for anyone watching and tossed it into the small waste tank under his workbench along with what was left of his sanitizer solution. After stepping on the flush lever, the star disappeared into the green. Tied above it, the red plastic ball bobbed for a moment, spinning around a vortex until it vanished after one last desperate bob to the surface.

"All right, Myron. Your turn," Rolf bellowed. Myron's head jerked up, his eyes transfixed on the swirling pool of green liquid. Rolf motioned to his assistant who snapped to his side to help him process Myron's work for the shift.

Behind the musical clank of gears and gold plunking into bins, Myron stood on his toes, trying to get a look over Rolf, searching for Sindra, trying to catch a glimpse of her face, read whether she had seen or heard Rolf's ruckus at Myron's bench earlier, but her back was already turned, waiting for exit procedures.

"Five wooley, Myron," Rolf stated, stacking five wooden tokens embossed with the industrial hammer seal on the table, coins so worn their centers were pocked with craters about the size of a rubbing thumb.

All his daydreaming and work on the star and the God-forgotten pinch of that fishing bob scraping his insides had cost Myron productivity. The last worker out, he stopped at an arched door. Martha, who made sure everyone who had entered the factory also exited, straddled the stool by the doorway, her limbs narrow and fallow, almost indistinguishable from the legs on the stool. "Come on," she barked. "Night shift is waiting."

Myron entered the cloakroom visualizing the contours of Sindra's face, the corners of her mouth that seemed to point upward, a smile where there was none, a splinter of clear blue threatening to punch through the festering sky. His anticipation of seeing her outside the walls of the factory, free from Rolf's big eye, gave him a flutter in his stomach instead of the usual hunger pangs.

He raised his hands over his head, opened his mouth and moved his tongue from side to side. Rolf gave the hand torch a few cranks and aimed the beam of light into Myron's mouth, yanking Myron's cheek open for a deep look, a sensation he shared with the fish that got hooked in his grandfather's stories. Then he bent over for the cavity check, the same procedure every day, all to quash *loss of product*.

"Go on," the ghost by the door barked, giving Myron a swat in the ribs with a discipline rod. The incoming foreman, Rolf's replacement on the night shift, glared at Myron as though the day shifters were inferior salvagers.

Dreading the chill that awaited him on the other side of the door, Myron snatched his pants from the hook and pulled them on. He slid his feet into his leather slips and wrapped up in a black smock. As the door creaked open, the next shift, night shifters, shivered in the cold, hopping from foot to foot, arms wrapped around their rib cages, hugging themselves for warmth. Light flurries began to fall, snow that bore a closer resemblance to frozen ash than anything white and wet. Myron felt the prick of the cold wind through the holes in his pants. He stood his collar up and buried his head in his smock, exposing his midriff to the bite of frozen air outside.

The orange haze of dusk stung his eyes. He dusted his eyelids free of all the tiny crumbs that accumulated during his shift and gazed at the return path to Jonesbridge, taking shallow breaths as his lungs filled with the stink of sulfur and magnesium. The familiar skyline of smokestacks disappeared into the haze, but as long as they continued to belch black clouds into the sky, hopes stayed alive that the war could be won.

Myron waited for a bicycle courier to pass him on the path, then checked over his shoulder for anyone else in sight. When he was confident he was alone, he snuck down the bank to the drainage canal's edge, a tributary of the Yarin Canal that drained the muck of the entire complex, taking it all the way to the Great Jonesbridge Gorge. Myron tried to get his footing but slipped partway on a slick of oil and sludge that almost sent him into the water headfirst.

In the canal, a green current swirled through black slicks. He followed the bank in the direction of the salvage factory, his eyes scanning for the red fishing bob that would hopefully carry the star he made for Sindra. Under a brick archway of the factory outtake, where the odor of the chemicals in the sanitizer overpowered the sulfur in the air, Myron spotted the red float, snagged on the wall, being tugged under by the current of nearby turbines. He squeezed his eyes shut and dipped his foot into the water, imagining how much it would mean to Sindra to get a gift like that star, real metal, *personal* metal.

He swatted for the bob, slapping and reaching, trying to free it until he got a hand on it, lifting it to check for weight. The metal points from the star pierced the surface of the water, and *Sindra's Star* dangled from the end of the string, wet and twinkling as it spun.

Myron's teeth chattered so hard that his jaw hurt. He could no longer feel the skin on his legs, and if he could have seen them, his smiling lips would have been blue. Seized by a fit of coughing, he flopped out onto the bank, holding the star above his head, the rush of icy wind stinging his skin.

Across the canal, on the embankment, a mumbling voice interupted the hum of the turbines. A ghost dragged someone to the water's edge. As they grew closer, Myron inched back into the muck, rolling himself into a ball for warmth, stifling his cough to keep quiet.

"Elements got the better of this one?" A guard shouted, tapping his discipline rod against the ground as he approached.

"Elements? Yeah, that's one way to put it. Caught this one duty shirking behind the number five coal shed."

On the verge of a sneeze, Myron swallowed hard to keep it down. He slapped his hand over his nose, and the chemical stench from his fingers made the canal bank spin. He could feel the thump of his heart between his toes, between the intermittently numb and stinging flesh on his ankles.

"Croaked?" The ghost asked, giving the body a nudge.

The other ghost drew back his discipline rod and thwacked the slog in the middle of his head. Myron winced, hearing the crack of the hard wood against the man's skull

"If he wasn't croaked before, he is now. This one's a relic. Wouldn't survive the stretcher anyway."

Myron panicked. If caught hunkered on the bank of the Yarin, they might mistake *him* for a duty shirker, and he wasn't sure he had fully recovered from his last stretch during orientation. He pressed farther into the muck and watched the two ghosts heave the shirker into the canal.

After a splash, the body rolled in the lazy current and its face turned towards Myron. Martino the barber, who had branded every arriving slog for the past thirty years, the oldest man in Jonesbridge, drifted along the green slime—

flushed down the Yarin Canal.

With the wind at his face, Myron trudged to his domicile through flurries of brown snow and ash. Wet pants against his skin burned as he made his way along the path, thoughts of Sindra driving each step.

CHAPTER 3

Still wet and raw from the cold wind, Myron stumbled to the commissary for Housing Block Fourteen C. The dull bricks of the unit rose in contrast to the graying evening sky behind it. His stomach growled. Even the petrified wooden "rations" sign swinging on leather straps looked appetizing. The thought hadn't struck him before, but staring at that sign, he wondered if leather—being that it came from an animal—had any protein and if it could fill the stomach in a pinch. He'd come close to testing that theory today, but as hungry as he was, he couldn't stop thinking about Sindra.

Everything about her was different—the way she walked with a little skip in her step, and when she spoke, her words sounded as though she pulled them from a quiver and aimed them right at him. She was special. He'd known it the first time he saw her, kicking her escorts, fighting every step, and that spirit had inspired him to someday figure a way out of Jonesbridge no matter the risk.

Myron had looked forward to seeing Sindra all day, but not with his hair a mess and canal slime dripping from his smock. After he procured his daily ration of two protein sticks and a rye biscuit, he headed across the block commons to the stairs, trying to avoid her until he could clean up. Four flights, nearly eighty steps of enduring wet burlap on flesh as the stairwell tunneled the wind right through the fabric. On the third floor, teeth chattering, Myron passed the familiar faded poster of the mustachioed Superintendent of Industry, young and fit, standing two heads taller than his fellow workers, overlooking a cauldron of molten iron. The posters in Jonesbridge had no words, and it hadn't taken Myron long to figure out why. Slogs couldn't read, except for him, which made it doubly important for him to hide his secret.

On the fourth floor he stepped between two ghosts on patrol, and he braced for a swat from the rod. He made his way down a narrow corridor lined on both sides with doors, stopping at number seventeen. The door creaked open as he leaned on the handle.

Myron let his soaking pants slump around his ankles as he entered his quarters. He stoked the dying embers in his stove with the rest of his coal ration, his body still shivering. Within seconds, his pants, socks and coat, were draped from the stove like sails on a ship, conjuring the image of a merchant vessel from a faraway ocean, docking in his quarters with the spoils of exploration on display.

All workers at his level, at least those in Fourteen C, shared a common urinal and resided in chambers not much longer than a cot, and about as wide. Each domicile had a small terra cotta stove, a basin, and a cot, which was too short since Myron was taller than most. Occupying an inside corner of the fourth floor, his room had no window, which meant less of the choking sulfur smell to penetrate his room and probably a warmer winter than those on the outside corridor with an opening to dissipate the heat.

With the chill in his bones gone, Myron stood at the basin checking his hair in the mirror, ducking his head from side to side trying to get just the right angle to find an untarnished spot in the reflection. He polished his teeth with his finger and spat. Then he dipped his hands in a bag of sealing wax and slicked his jet-black hair back on his head before he grabbed the star he had made for Sindra and plopped down on his cot.

From behind a section of loose bricks where he kept his personal contraband items, mostly the books he got from his grandfather, Myron grabbed the postcard of Bora Bora, the farthest reaches of the earth, the final destination of his great escape.

Myron lit the wick on his last candle in this month's ration. A flicker of yellow splashed across the pages in the *Atlas of the Modern World*, one of only two ancient books he possessed. He enjoyed locating himself and anywhere else he knew about in the context of the Old Age, and Jonsebridge he determined was a point near two regions titled New Mexico and Utah. His favorite maps were details of grand cities once connected by a web of travelways that spanned the entire continent, but he never cracked the book without eventually finding Bora Bora. It was nothing more than a spec in a tiny archipelago, so remote, so far out in the middle of the greatest ocean on earth that Myron could imagine spending the rest of his life just getting there.

Down the corridor, doors slammed over the grating tenor of Rolf's voice. "Day shift contraband inspection!" As the foreman for day shift salvage, Rolf also had the duty of making sure his slogs conformed to the standards of Industry, and he made his inspections irregular enough to be a surprise.

Myron hopped to his feet as he heard the muffled sounds of his fellow slogs shuffling outside. He couldn't breathe. The star. Sindra's star. Of all times to have a domicile inspection, he was holding enough personal metal to be considered aiding the enemy.

"We're missing one," a voice shouted.

"Myron," Rolf called from the quad commons. "Out!"

Myron yanked his cot back, groping the wall until he reached the set of loose bricks to stow his book. The bricks tumbled out onto the floor. He usually had more time to arrange them perfectly, to return each brick and strip of mortar to its place.

"Go drag his ass out of there," Rolf shouted. "Wait. I'll do it."

Myron rolled up the book and shoved it into its spot in the wall. The postcard he tucked into his smock. When he tried to cram in the star, the bricks didn't assemble right. In his hurry, he couldn't get the fishing float to fit in either.

Heavy footsteps fell outside his door.

Without thinking, he arranged the bricks in the wall and threw the star along with the bob into the stove. Then he stuck his hand in and pulled a white-hot coal over the star to hide it. He bit his lip to stifle a scream; the pain of the coals on his skin almost made him lose his lights.

The fishing bob melted into a red blob on top of the

coals. He would now have to find a new way to smuggle metal out of the salvage factory. Hopefully, a less painful method.

The door swung open.

"I'm sorry," Myron said, rushing out into the corridor. "I burned my hand. Stoking the fire. Didn't hear the inspection." He put on his best empty gaze and showed Rolf his hand.

Rolf cracked a thin smile. "Don't even have sense enough to use your stoker." He strolled through Myron's room, lifted the cot, peaked behind the stove, and tapped the walls randomly, until his eyes narrowed. "Whore's hairpin, what's that smell?" Rolf wrinkled up his nose. He threw his head back, sniffing the air.

Myron smelled it, too, coming from the stove. The fishing bob, "Just a lump of funny coal in my ration. Piece of brittle," Myron said, playing stupid.

"Brittle?" Rolf grabbed Myron's ceramic stoker and poked the coals. A strand of melted red string stuck to the end and followed the poker out of the fire. "What a mess. What are you up to? Making that funny gear this morning. Burning brittle in your stove." Rolf turned on his heel at the door. "There's something not right about you, boy." He tossed Myron's stoker on his cot and walked out.

Myron checked down the corridor to make sure the inspection team had moved on and fished the star out of the fire. He tore a piece off of his smock and wrapped his burned fingers. After getting dressed, he checked his hair again and put on his coat along with his dour, moronic public face before heading for his ration.

As he came to the bottom of the stairs, he ducked under the low archway that opened into the swill pen, what slogs in quad 14 called the stagnant courtyard bound by their four domicile buildings. Under a string of dim bulbs that stretched from the staircases of 14A to 14C, day shifters sat on benches around the chimney of a crumbling brick kiln and gnawed the only food they would get for the day. Most ate in silence, too tired to speak. Others murmured of the war and whatever news the Superintendent had offered during his daily admonition. A few slogs huddled in the dark corner conducting a discreet game of nub, played with four worn stones on a grid drawn in the dirt, with rations as the prize. Myron searched the crowd until his eyes found Sindra, who sat on bench eating her ration alone.

They glanced at each other briefly. Under the cones of yellow light, Sindra's delicate features betrayed the defiance in her eyes, a quality that had inspired Myron from the moment he first saw her. And every time their eyes had met since, his stomach jumped with excitement. Her spirit was bigger than Jonesbridge. Mystery surrounded her as though she guarded a secret. She even looked different, healthier than the rest of them. Most slogs were torpid and gaunt, racks of bones with skin stretched over them, but Sindra had some color in her cheeks. She had curves, even a wiggle of extra flesh on her backside.

Myron sat on the bench a few feet away from her and whispered, as if talking to himself, "I looked for you today. When Rolf was riding me."

Sindra stared across the swill pen away from Myron. "I saw you looking," she whispered, concealing her smile.

Her comment stoked his worry that she might have seen the star when Rolf held it up, which would spoil the surprise. Myron studied the faces around him, all occupied with their rations. He scooted a little closer to Sindra though he kept his gaze on the ghosts pacing by the staircases. "What's wrong?" Sindra's face usually became more animated when she was with Myron.

"Can't sleep," she said as if to no one.

"Why not?"

Sindra opened her mouth to speak but took a bite of bread instead, waiting for a slog to walk past. "I can't take this."

"What?"

"What they do."

Myron scooted closer.

"Wish I'd catch the wet lung if it meant they'd leave me be."

Myron studied her face as she spoke, hoping for a glimpse of the untamed girl he had grown accustomed to. Her inner fire fueled his; he was certain that he would shrivel away if this place had robbed Sindra of her spirit.

"Never thought I'd miss the tracks. The smell of tar and rockweed and the rail-walking vagrants with turnip breath. I guess I was sheltered from the bigger world and all its problems." Sindra moved over on the bench casting Myron an admonishing glare.

Myron knew the rules. *Industry slogs of opposite gender must not commingle alone.* This mandate also applied to slogs of the same gender should such proclivities exists between them. He scooted over on the bench, to the very edge, squeezing his hand around the star.

"I have to get out of this place," Sindra whispered.

Myron had trusted Sindra from the first time he had seen her, but in recent weeks she had reciprocated the trust by opening up to Myron about her past. "I know where we can meet. Away from here, at least for a little while," Myron whispered. The spot was an abandoned chapel with crumbling wooden walls and remnants of stained glass. The roof sunk almost to the tops of the pews in places. The only problem, it stood well beyond the slog compound perimeter, a boundary only legally crossed by ghosts on patrol.

"Meet—as in alone?"

"Yes."

The abandoned chapel, now swallowed up by needle grass and briar vine, stood in the shadow of Iron's Knob. Myron pointed to the promontory shrouded in smoke nearly five hects away, the most prominent landmark inside the area bound by the Great Gorge. On one side a gently sloping hill and dry creek bed, the other a jagged cliff face that made Iron's Knob resemble the tip of a pickaxe blade jutting out of the ground.

"Outside the compound? No way." Sindra shook her head.

He understood her apprehension with nightmares of the stretcher always in the back of his mind, but her reaction disappointed him. Myron imagined a rail-walker like Sindra—a scrapper who fought with orange shirts the first day she arrived—would jump at a chance for adventure. Unless she didn't feel he was worth the risk.

"Don't worry, I go all the time."

Her eyes grew wide. "If we can we get out of the compound, why stop at the chapel?"

Myron had the same thought when he first ventured beyond the compound. "Not possible. Legend doesn't pay that gorge its due. No way across. No way through. Only one way—and that's over." He glided his hand through the air.

"So how do we get past the ghosts on patrol?"

Then he saw it, the same look in her eyes he had seen when she bit that ghost on the arm five months ago, a glint, as though her eyes laughed at the thought of getting caught.

"Only if you don't mind getting dirty," Myron said.

"Myron, if you land me another minute in that stretcher for this," Sindra whispered. After a moment, she looked at him in a way that Myron took for interest, and then she nodded.

"There's a wooden grate on the ground behind 14-B," he pointed to the domiciles across the commons. "An abandoned maintenance tunnel. The ghosts don't even know it's there, but we'll have to go one at a time." Myron had grown comfortable with the risk, confident that he had memorized the patrol patterns. He knew how much time he had to get through the grate and get it covered again. Adding an extra, uninitiated person doubled the risk. "Are you sure?"

Her face glowed with anticipation. "Yes."

Myron glanced at the crowd gathered in the commons, gnawing on rations and swapping stories about another work day on the salvage line. Two ghosts strolled in front of 14-B. "There they go. After they cross, count to thirty, stand up, and walk to the stairs for 14-B. Make sure nobody notices you. Then sneak behind the building."

Sindra's eyebrows narrowed as she eyed the commons, an open courtyard bound on four sides by Quad 14's domiciles, with only one opening where the brick path of the commons joined the main road to the factories.

Myron counted as another ghost emerged from the

fourth floor corridor with a clear view of the area behind the building. "If you're not out of sight by then, you got problems."

Sindra's lips tightened into a straight line. "Got it. Where is the grate exactly?"

"Right under where the catcher net starts." Myron hated the suicide nets that circled the building just above the first floor, put in place for the higher floors. The need for their existence reminded him more of his drudgery than extra shifts on no rations. If there was one crime the Superintendent of Industry harped on in his admonitions more than duty shirking, it was suicide: the ultimate shirk. *The selfish, unpatriotic, treasonous act of unilaterally removing a producing slog from the line*, was a decision no slog was allowed to make. *Sacrifice now, rejoice later. There will be plenty of time for the betterment of life when the war is won.*

Myron scooted farther over from Sindra on the bench when he noticed Saul looking their way. Saul stood with his hands behind his back surveying the swill pen the same way the ghosts did, except that Saul was a slog, and lower in seniority than most of the slogs in quad 14. He made everyone's business his business.

"Saul is as bad as the ghosts," Myron said under his breath. "So don't move from this bench if there's a chance he's watching you."

"Wait. What do I do when I get there?"

"Move the grate aside, hop down and slide the grate back over. I'll go first. That way I'll be there."

Myron glanced at Sindra. Her eyes, peculiar and round, the same color as shin pine needles, absorbed their surroundings as if she had seen the swill pen for the first time.

That look made him forget all dangers—that he might be being watched—and he leaned over and kissed her, nothing more than a peck, but it surprised them both so much that Myron did not look back for her reaction. Instead, he stood and waited for the ghosts on patrol. When the time came, he made his way for the tunnel.

CHAPTER 4

Hunkered down in the crawlway of the abandoned tunnel—with only a sliver of light from the grate—reminded Myron of hiding from the orange shirts when they came for him as a kid. Holed up in the potato pantry where it stank of mildew and soil, his knees up against his nose, his mother insisting to the Civil Guards that she had no children. When they discovered her lie, his mom fought them until they buried a vegetable hatchet into her forehead. The blood on the kitchen floor was still fresh in Myron's mind.

He waited, patiently at first, biting his fingernails, counting the correct number of seconds to time the patrols. As all the things that could go wrong paraded across his mind, he lost count—and his train of thought. Panic settled in. Two patrols had passed and no Sindra.

Above him, boots marched over the grate—the third patrol since he had arrived. A few moments later, he heard another set of softer foot falls.

"Myron," Sindra whispered from above the grate.

"Down here." All the tensed muscles in his body relaxed at once. With one hand on the rusted ladder, he wiggled a finger through the grate and slid it aside. "Hurry."

Sindra hopped into the hole, landing in Myron's arms. "Saul kept watching me," she whispered through heavy breaths. "What is this place?" She rubbed her hand along the darkening wall, tapping at a box with red and yellow buttons permanently pressed inward as Myron refitted the tunnel cover overhead.

"My guess, a maintenance tunnel. From the Old Age. Looks like when they salvaged all the useable metal out of it," Myron said, making a crunching noise, "the whole thing collapsed right in on itself." He looked ahead into the darkness that concealed a network of twisted crawl spaces and air pockets. "I've seen one other grate, one like this one, over by the salvage factory, but I've never been able to get close enough to it."

Myron groped for a hand-crank flashlight similar to what Rolf used during exit procedures, something he had unearthed in an old bunker near the Gorge. He cranked the flashlight a few times, and a yellow beam splashed across the rocks ahead. "Come on."

They crept through the tunnel, sliding into openings and twisting through sagging chunks of earth and concrete. Myron felt Sindra's hand on his back, tethered to him all the way, until the gray light of dusk filtered through the lattice on the entry hatch ahead. The opening on the chapel end of the tunnel had a heavier, hinged cover that creaked when Myron swung it open, and they emerged at the foot of a bell tower, long robbed of its bell, standing guard over the ruins of an old chapel.

Tramping through patches of gray snow, Myron led Sindra under a collapsed doorway that opened into the vestibule of a forgotten world. On the south side of the building, a stone wall crumbled beneath the splintered remains of an ornate roof trestle. On the north side was a row of arching windows that would have once diced sunlight into iridescent shards through panes of stained glass. Scant remnants of the windows lived on in glittery patches in the soil, but nothing remained intact to keep the icy wind at bay.

When Sindra first saw the chapel, she twirled, and her smock rose high around her waist. Just seeing her smile made the trip worth the risk for Myron. She continued to explore the chapel with the flashlight as though it were her new home, peering under the pews, checking the view out the windows. She ran her fingers across the carvings on the petrified altar that stood half-buried in needle vine at the front of the sanctuary. With both arms spread like a bird making an unsure landing, she glided from the altar to the front row of seats and sat on the pew. After a glance over her shoulder, a habit every slog in Jonesbridge developed in time, she dug through a fold on the inside of her smock and pulled out a length of pork strap and ripped a hunk off with her teeth.

"Where'd you get that?" Myron's mouth watered.

"I don't want to talk about it. If I think about *that* I'll lose my appetite. Here, you take the rest."

Myron wondered how far he would go for extra rations. Some nights, in a fit of delirium, his blood low on sugars, he fantasized about breaking the window out of the commissary and raiding the place, shoveling everything he passed into his open mouth and then getting so sloshed on rot-onion and rye he would forget what he had done. He came close a month ago, after a double shift on reduced rations.

"What happened to your fingers?" Sindra reached for Myron's burned hand.

He grabbed his hand to hide the burlap strip and fidgeted for a moment before he looked into her eyes and placed the star he had made for her in her hand.

Sindra glanced down at the shape, her eyes, her entire face lifted when she held out the star. She turned it over and ran her finger along the inscription. "What does it say?"

"Sindra's Star."

"Old Nickel—she was sort of a mom to the rail-walkers—used to say that stars are anchors for the soul." She gave him a hug. Myron couldn't remember the last time he had hugged someone, bodies connecting for a time, as though her softer parts dulled the edges of his bones.

"Look, Myron," Sindra fought back tears. "I—I don't think I can make it in Jonesbridge. We've made it this far. Let's keep going."

Myron often felt that way when he came to the chapel. Sneaking out of the compound granted a sense of freedom, but the only boundary that mattered, the Great Gorge, dug to keep the enemy at bay, imprisoned the workers of Jonesbridge by surrounding them with an impassable crevasse spanned by only one highly guarded bridge. The Great Gorge began as a natural oxbow lake dug ever deeper and wider—deep enough for midday darkness, or so the legend went—where all of the noxious muck of Jonesbridge drained. "The Gorge," Myron said with a sigh.

"Okay then, why can't we just stay out here—on

the fringe?"

Myron took Sindra's hand and turned it over to look at her tattoos. "You're an Industry slog now, and if you get caught out here, you're not some rail-walker wild woman anymore. You're a duty shirker. And a traitor to the Alliance." Myron thought of Martino floating in the canal, fighting the image of Sindra facedown in green froth. "And there's nothing to eat. No clean water. No nothing out here."

Not much would grow in the barren shadows of the mountains, at least nothing edible, but what did grow pricked the feet and shins with spiny outgrowths and thorns. Their branches, except in the case of the shin pines, bore nothing but fingernail-sized brown leaves in the spring, the only thing distinguishing them from the razor wire encircling the commissary roof to keep out would-be thieves. Everything else, old-timers called shin pines, which were really pinyon pines stunted by the toxic soil keeping them from growing much higher than a man's leg—just tall enough to scrape the shins.

On the other side of the Gorge, the tops of the surrounding hills and mountains had been completely removed, strip-mined all the way to a smooth layer of rocks, making the scrub and briars on the hills in the Jonesbridge valley look like beard stubble on the otherwise smooth face of the countryside.

"Come on, Myron. Let's go as far as we can. I'm a rail-walker. I can scrounge."

The same thought had crossed Myron's mind earlier as he reconsidered accelerating his escape plan. "I've been planning a way out of here. Maybe we could go now, but I think I need more time."

"I don't have time. Things are bad for me." Sindra stared right into his eyes. "Where would we go?"

Myron had a hard time imagining how she had it any worse than he did. She even managed extra rations. Her defiant spirit had little tolerance for captivity. He sat down beside her, almost convinced to make a run for it now, and dug into his smock for his prized postcard of Bora Bora.

"That's beautiful." Sindra's eyes widened.

"It's a postcard note. People in the Old Age used to send each other keepsakes when they journeyed to faraway places." The picture on the card had faded, the colors had grayed, but underneath the crisscrossing veins of wear was a photograph of a beach with a single arching palm tree. "That's where I'm headed. Bora Bora."

"I wonder what it says." Sindra leaned over Myron's shoulder until she could feel her curves on his back.

Myron hesitated, having kept his ability to read secret for so long. "Our flight was delayed in Los Angeles. We had to take a puddle jumper from Tahiti, but we're finally here in paradise. I've already got you a souvenir mask. I hope you're minding your grandmother. P.S. Eat your green beans."

"It's so amazing that you can read." Sindra scooted farther toward him until their legs touched. "Can you teach me?"

"Yeah, maybe."

"Los Angeles?" She took the postcard. "The broken city at the bottom of the sea?"

"I don't know about anywhere else. Only Bora Bora. That's where I'm headed."

"It's wondrous."

"That's why I need more time. When I go—when *we*

go," he corrected, unable to hide the blush he felt on his cheeks, "it has to be *over* the Gorge." He sailed his hand through the air. "That's the only way out of here."

"Over?"

Myron nodded, as Sindra's face twisted into a doubtful pout. "I'm building a flying machine. An airship like my grandfather's."

"What, exactly, is an airship?" Her lips pursed, and her eyes narrowed.

Myron could explain what an airship was, but he had no words to convey the sensation of flying, something he had experienced only once, when he was twelve. Up over Richterville, over the village chimneys, each one with a trail of gray like hundreds of mouths blowing out pipe smoke. The air had been thick with brown and gray from nearby factories until they breeched the smoke where the air felt like a gossamer sheet, as though a sky that clear might shatter like a pane of glass with the slightest noise. That day his grandfather explained that a balloon only goes where the wind takes it. An airship, with its rudder and propeller, goes where the pilot takes it.

Before he could answer Sindra, Myron heard what sounded like a crunch of footsteps on dry brush. A shiver ran up his neck. He held his finger to his lips.

As he turned around, a hand grabbed his arm with as much force as a pressure clamp. Myron squeezed his eyes shut, preparing for a paralyzing blow from a discipline rod. Instead, a body, furry and damp, pressed against his back, wrenching his arm until his shoulder throbbed. A blast of hot breath hit the nape of his neck. It smelled of rotting flesh and excrement, turning Myron's stomach. In a low whisper that sounded like wind on a window pane, a voice said, "I'll tell you what an airship is."

Sindra gasped and jumped behind a far pew.

Night had fallen, and without the flashlight, the only light that remained was the distant reflection of the factory lamps off the low blanket of smoke overhead. Myron jerked his arm, hoping to break free. Unable to make out the man who had materialized in front of him, Myron saw only gray and brown fur with patches of hide, making it impossible to tell where the fur stopped and the man's beard began. The furrowed skin surrounding his eyes was the only part of his face not swallowed by hair. Hoping the wild man standing before him had already eaten and had no designs on human flesh, Myron backed away. "Who are you?"

"Me? I'm a coyote," the man proclaimed. "What you hill monkeys call a goat fox. Only creature left that's crafty enough to survive in this rotten land."

"Goat foxes don't talk."

"I wasn't born a coyote." The hairs in his beard flared when he spoke, but Myron could not see a mouth. "But I became one. When they took me in and let me live among 'em." He gave a yip and howl that mimicked the sounds that came from the rim at night.

Myron had heard goat foxes called coyotes before. His grandfather had said that they could drink brackish water and eat cockroaches if it came down to survival, but he'd never met a person claiming to be one.

The man pointed to the Great Gorge. "I know what you're up to, boy." He poked his finger into Myron's chest and twisted in Sindra's direction. "I see you over there too, girly."

Sindra ducked behind the pew, out of sight.

"I used to call that bunker home. Till it started filling up with garbage. Same as every other damn place. Garbage and smoke." He reached over the pew and grabbed Sindra, pulling her up by her hair. Sindra grunted, twisting and kicking to break free. "This slippery fellow is building some sort of flying contraption." He poked Myron again in the chest.

Myron's heart sank. His secret, the fate of all his plans, now rested on the whims of a kook who thought himself a coyote. Myron elbowed the man in the ribs and jerked free. Seizing her opportunity, Sindra kicked him in the knee and twisted loose. "Run!" Myron shouted. Sindra broke into the shadows of the vestibule, and Myron ran the other way, hoping to confuse the Coyote Man.

"You're not flying anywhere without *me*!" The man yelled.

Coyote Man snatched him by the smock as Myron jumped into the dry creek bed that ran beside the chapel. His smock ripped, but he worked himself loose. Coyote Man tumbled into the creek bed behind Myron, groping for a handhold.

"Come back here."

Staying in a crouched position, Myron jogged along the creek and hopped out near the tunnel opening where Sindra, still out of breath, waited with a rock in her hand. The rusty hinges on the tunnel hatch squealed when Myron eased it open. He scanned the darkness for any signs of Coyote Man, wondering if he'd heard the noise. As soon as the hatch opened, Sindra climbed down into the collapsed tunnel ahead of Myron.

Keeping as quiet as possible, Myron held his hand out

and nodded at the star he'd given Sindra. She shook her head, but Myron insisted. He didn't want to leave it here, but she couldn't risk having it in her domicile. He dug a hole in the dirt to hide it.

Myron entered the tunnel first, feeling his way until he could safely use the flashlight where Coyote Man wouldn't notice any flashes of light. Sindra followed, her body pressed up against his. Their pace slowed as they navigated the jagged tunnel where the narrow openings required them to crawl. Sindra knew all his secrets now—Bora Bora, his flying machine—but so did that Coyote Man. Knowing he was out there, running free on the fringes of Jonesbridge, made Myron fearful for his plan.

When they reached the grate behind the domicile quad, Myron stowed his flashlight behind the ladder, and the tunnel faded into darkness. He stared into the black for a while, listening for movement in the tunnel, any signs that they were followed.

"You're not like other people," Sindra whispered.

As he turned around, she kissed him, a long kiss, their lips pressed together, the way he imagined two people might kiss if they were paired for mating, a silent vow that strengthened Myron's resolve to get them both out of Jonesbridge.

Myron took a deep breath, now more cautious than ever. "Can't risk going together. You go first. I'll go after the ghosts go by, so I can get the grate back on."

Myron waited and listened for the ghosts on patrol. After they passed, he opened the cover and made a stirrup with his hands for Sindra to step in, then heaved her up though the opening. A gust of frosty wind whipped her hair as she crawled onto the ground. Sindra looked over her shoulder at

Myron. The hem of her burlap smock twirled as she hopped to her feet. Their eyes met, and Myron waved her on, already in mid-count to estimate when the ghosts would return.

Moments after he closed the grate, inches away from his nose, a dark blob suddenly obstructed his view. He recognized the shape of it, a boot heel square in the middle of the grate, now two; only ghosts wore boots. Myron's hands trembled as a wave of numbness traveled the length of this body, hoping Sindra had managed to make it out of sight. He couldn't figure why the ghosts hadn't followed their routine. They should have moved on by now.

"Oh, it's my lucky night," the voice over the grate said. Myron saw the smudge of a hand grab Sindra's arm. "I don't even have to share you tonight."

The ghost muffled Sindra's scream with his hand right before she bit it. Myron pressed on the grate, now sealed by the weight of the ghost and Sindra.

"Get off me," Sindra hissed. There was a shuffle of feet and fabric rippling, but he heard the struggle, and then Myron caught a glimpse of Sindra's eyes, sad and submissive, the wild in them defeated.

Myron heard rustling and snorts and grunts. When he heard Sindra's voice, his insides churned. He had seen a lot of things in Jonesbridge, but he realized then that he hadn't seen the one thing that never even crossed a slog's mind—which was why Sindra had it so bad.

Myron pushed on the grate, not sure what he would do if the grate actually lifted. With the weight of Sindra and the ghost, the wooden grid didn't budge. Ripping burlap preceded a flap of loose fabric that billowed across the grate, revealing flashes of Sindra's bare flesh through the grid. After a slap of hands on skin, Myron caught bits of a leg, her midriff, and then a part of Sindra's body, her gender, that Myron shouldn't have seen. The ghost's pants slumped around his ankles, and Sindra's body raised as she screamed and pleaded.

Hearing the ghost's grunts, Myron squeezed his eyes shut. Coyote Man or not, he still had faith in his plan to escape Jonesbridge, and now his plan included Sindra. He conjured the image of waves breaking on the shore near an arching palm tree with Sindra under it smiling. Behind her, the grass from the hut, just like the one on the postcard, fluttered with the ocean breeze. No smoke, no war, no toil, only he and Sindra and what remained of the grand beasts of the ocean. Myron had stifled his tears as a silent witness the day his mother died, but now, he took a deep breath and heaved against the grate, this time cracking it.

"What the..." The ghost yelled.

Again, Myron slammed against the grate with enough force to knock the ghost, with lowered pants, off balance. The grate popped up from the ground. The ghost and Sindra fell against the rear wall of the domicile quad. Myron emerged from the tunnel with the heavy wooden grate in hand and whipped the ghost's head with it hard enough to knock him off of Sindra, who lay on the ground with her legs pulled apart. Myron looked away. Blood trickled from the ghost's head.

"Are you okay?" Myron picked up the ripped fabric and tried to cover Sindra's exposed areas. "I didn't know they—"

"They take whatever they want," Sindra sobbed.

Myron held his hand to her mouth and pointed toward voices.

Sindra shook her head and pointed to the tunnel.

Myron showed her the wooden grate that had splintered in half, "Run, Sindra." He pushed her toward the quad. "Before he wakes up." Behind them, they heard the ghosts on patrol.

CHAPTER 5

Myron shuffled along with the crowd. He hadn't yet spotted Sindra this morning, and he could hardly wait to see her on the factory floor. Considering he made it back to his domicile and had not yet been apprehended, he felt confident the ghost he struck hadn't seen his face. But he worried about Sindra, whether the ghosts would blame her.

As he approached the salvage factory, Myron observed a peculiar blue swatch of sky. No one else seemed to notice, trudging down the path, heads down, but the smokestacks burned a little lighter today than usual, allowing striations of sunlight to pierce the haze. Almost late for his shift already, he paused to enjoy the sight, knowing it wouldn't last.

At 7:00 A.M. the factory siren wailed from atop a stanchion in the salvage yard. It emitted a prolonged howl, hiccupped, and then ebbed into a moan, distinguishable from an attack warning only by the length of the interval. The day shift began this way, as the night shift ended, every day, seven days a week without exception.

Ninety-nine workers, already in place on the factory floor, stood at attention, arms straight down, chests out, eyes focused on the flag that hung like a tapestry on the towering south wall. Myron shuffled through the human pillars to fill the remaining empty workplace farthest away from the door, ears tuned to the audio box that hung from the ceiling. The anthem began just as Myron got into position. As the thunderous drums rolled in ahead of a chorus of bugles, all one hundred workers were accounted for.

Following a customary minute of silence, the Superintendent of Industry began his admonition for the shift, a communication that began with high-pitched feedback, followed by a wave of static, as though his words traveled through a field of broken glass before reaching the speaker.

"It saddens me to report that late last night, while our farmers slept, our enemy launched a surprise attack on the northern farms, devastating our last tract of untainted farmland anywhere north of Simonville."

A subdued chatter filled the work floor. Myron remembered the proud moment four months ago when the Superintendent referred to the narrow swath of clean ground only recently discovered.

"In your mirror this morning," the Industry Superintendent continued, "you saw the nose, eyes, ears and mouth—the face of our body. We are diminished now by hundreds—all citizens like you, lost last evening at the hands of our enemies. Your expression in that mirror, on the street, in the factory, is our reflection. If you are smiling, you are informing your world that you are happy," again he paused, a silence that filled with air like a balloon, until it finally popped. "Happy that hundreds of your fellow citizens are now gone? Satisfied with your production on the line? Gleeful that every moment you grin, someone else's life hinges on your job? Today is not a happy day." The voice disappeared again beneath a blanket of static and half-words before the box went silent.

Myron surveyed the expansive room at his fellow workers, relieved to see Sindra in her usual workspace. They all wore the austere countenance prescribed by the Superintendent of Industry, especially Sindra, who Myron imagined might never smile again. The fate of the *body* did weigh on Myron in the moments after the announcement, but he couldn't shake what happened last night. He could only watch Sindra listening to the daily admonition as though nothing had happened the night before.

Myron's grandfather had prayed often, and he told Myron that praying was once a common thing to do. People then, when his grandfather was a kid, prayed a lot, prayed for rain from the heavens, prayed for safety, prayed for peace and prosperity, for whatever need arose, especially in dire times. Myron wondered if each person had a predetermined number of answered prayers, somewhat like the number of tokens he made piecemeal every day, and if he exhausted his prayer tokens, when he required something from the Great Above later, when his very existence depended on it, would he have nothing left from which to draw his request?

He considered a prayer to keep his airship safe, prevent Coyote Man from finding it and destroying it in a fit of wild rage, but instead, he would ask from the Great Above that Sindra would never have to endure such a violation again.

He only had a few more supplies to gather, and now he would do whatever he had to do to get both of them over the gorge and on their way to Bora Bora.

Myron had assumed from the lengthy pause that the Superintendent had concluded his morning report, but a garbled wave of static broke the silence in the room. The Superintendent cleared his throat. "Last evening, one of our dutiful Civil Guards sacrificed his life in the line of duty for the Alliance." Myron had a sudden pain in his throat. "You owe your safety and comfort, your ability to work unhindered by fears of the enemy to the tireless efforts of our brave Civil Guard. Rest assured traitors are swiftly identified and exterminated."

The salvage floor erupted into gasps and murmurs. Myron couldn't breathe or swallow. A tingling sweat broke out on his forehead and he heard a faint ringing in his ears as though all of the blood in his body had suddenly gushed straight to his head. He rubbed his face, trying to focus. The sea of eyes across the room scanned from one slog to the next. He glanced at Sindra, and three workstations over, he noticed Saul staring at her too.

Myron tried to recall how hard he'd hit the ghost, seeing in his mind the oozing blood. Hearing that the ghost had died made him woozy and confused. When something happened to a ghost, nothing would stop them from getting to the truth. But no one, not even his fellow slogs, ever mentioned Martino's murder. There had been no announcement, no demand for justice for a common slog, only a ripple in the canal where Martino disappeared.

"Get to work," Rolf barked.

Myron had no idea how he could work today. His

hands trembled, he saw double, and his temples throbbed as if he had struck himself with a hammer, but he had no choice. With his tool bench positioned, he arranged his bins, preparing for a twelve-hour shift, all part of the rote mechanics of a job that began the same way every day, a process that continued with him yanking the lever above his head to sort through what came out. Gears, as usual, scrap, wires, a jumble of dull blades—Myron slipped on his gloves and gingerly spread the items, scanning for anything he could use on his airship. He had run out of time to gather materials for his escape, a flight that would have to happen now whether he was ready or not.

Unlike his fellow slogs, who bemoaned the drudgery of the factory floor, Myron marked his time putting together the puzzle of the present, and sometimes the past, based on the relics that crossed his bench. He admitted that most of it amounted to little more than battle debris and powder-fused mash-ups of twice recycled garbage, but every now and then another piece to the riddle of history fell onto his bench.

In his lot today, a curious square ceramic plate with two intact hinges. Stamped on it were the words *Biohazard, for genetic research purposes only* below a symbol with three incomplete circles leading from a red center circle. The hinges still functioned. It would make the perfect flue vent for regulating the coal fire in his airship's balloon, and since it wasn't metal, he could chuck it into the reprocess bin, which got dumped if the salvage admin saw no use for it. Myron would just have to fish it out of the outtake after his shift.

For twelve hours he fidgeted through his shift with panic building for any ensuing treason investigation, which would involve stretcher time for everyone. When his shift ended, his focus returned to his escape. He shuffled through exit procedures and out into the frigid air where flakes of ash and brown snow drifted by the door. As he watched his fellow slogs fill the path to 14-C, he scanned the area first to see who might be watching him and then slipped to the south side of the factory where the furnace slag dumped into the canal. He just had to keep an eye out for that bright red biohazard symbol with the three rings circumscribing a middle circle, and he would find his prize: the perfect flue vent.

Where Myron stood, close to the bank of the Yarin, the numbing breeze whipped through the endless corridor of red-bricked factory walls. His arms and legs ached. As the slag trickled down the chute, among the other debris, Myron reached for the hinged ceramic plate and quickly tucked it into his smock.

Seconds later, he felt the squeeze of a hand on his shoulder. He stopped breathing. This time he knew he had taken too many chances. The hand on his shoulder yanked him about, and instead of a ghost with a discipline rod poised over his head that he expected, Rolf stood, alone, eye to eye with Myron in the shadows of the salvage factory.

Nothing he could say would justify standing near the furnace chute where a rush of hot slag and slurry cascaded into the Yarin. Rolf thrust his elbow into Myron's throat, pressing his neck against the brick wall of the salvage factory. "What do you think you're doing back here?" Rolf said.

Myron couldn't swallow, could barely breathe. He tried to squirm free. Closer and closer to the furnace outtake, Rolf pushed Myron's head until he could feel droplets of hot slag on his face, almost losing his footing on the slope of the chute. Myron pulled away from the gray sludge with all his power. Losing his balance, he grabbed Rolf by the smock, and they fought to keep from tumbling into the outtake.

"I don't know what kind of game you're playing, but there's a way things are done around here and you ain't doing it. It's simple: You come to work. You process what ends up in your station. You keep your mouth shut. You leave work." Rolf glanced over his shoulder again. "You *don't* sneak around. You *don't* steal from the slag pit and you *don't* putter along like some sort of ape making doe eyes with that carpie."

"No, sir."

"I've noticed." Rolf straightened his smock and stood again up on his toes to be the same height as Myron. He thumped the industry tattoo on the back of his hand. "No one makes *choices* here. That's the way of the world."

Myron kept his eye on the furnace chute to keep from sliding down it. He stayed quiet, preserving his fate to muddle through another day in one piece.

"You think *they* don't watch me too? You slogs don't produce. I get the blame." Rolf made a fist and pummeled the soft spot under Myron's sternum, just above the hidden ceramic plate in his smock, an unexpected blow that doubled Myron over and emptied his winds. Rolf gave him another smack, this time on the head sending him to the frozen ground. "As sneaky as you are, it wouldn't surprise me if *you* were the one that upended that ghost."

Rolf's accusation took Myron off guard, allowing him no time to think. "No, no. No." Myron shook his head. No one would ever believe him that he hadn't meant to kill the guard or that the guard had it coming. "There's this wild man. Lives out on the rim." The words came to him like a gift from the Great Above, a way to shift the blame and save his airship from Coyote Man at the same time. "He's the one. I'll bet he did it."

"A wild man?" Rolf scoffed.

"When they find him, you'll see."

Rolf pointed a finger at Myron. "If you're making this up," he said, nodding to the slag trickling down the chute, "you're going out with the garbage." He grabbed Myron by the smock and hoisted him to his feet, giving him a shove between his shoulder blades to get him going. Relieved that the ceramic-hinged plate stayed out of sight during the scuffle, Myron returned to the path, hurrying to the domicile quad.

Back in the swill pen, at least six people hovered next to Saul, gnawing their rations, engaged in the most spirited conversation Myron had seen in his time in Jonesbridge. His stomach jumped when he noticed one of them was Sindra, and when their eyes met, she looked away.

"I'm not surprised something like this happened," Saul said, his eyes narrowing. "I've seen some strange things, lately." He glared right at Myron as he joined the group. His gaze then moved over to Sindra.

"What kind of things?" A woman asked. She worked textiles for their block, which meant fashioning burlap such that it could be worn. Myron rarely saw her, and when he did, he never heard her speak.

Still glaring at Sindra, Saul said, "I aim to figure out who this traitor is before we all get questioned in the stretcher. You think orientation was bad—"

An older, one-legged man limped on a crutch over to Saul. He pulled to a stop, face-to-face, like an ammo train butting up to a depot buffer. "If you're accusing someone, come right out with it."

Saul backed up, holding a hand up toward the one-legged man. "You're new to this quad. Makes you a suspect already. I'd keep quiet."

"A suspect," the textile woman scoffed. "He's a war veteran." She pointed to the man's missing leg.

"For all we know, he could've been born a gimp," Saul said.

The one-legged man lifted his burlap smock. A stump, severed at mid-thigh, dangled beneath his protruding pelvis. "Lost in some God-forgotten swamp to an E'ster piss whistle not six months ago." He reached down and tugged at his good leg as though he were mired in bog water. "Name's Errol, by the way."

The gathering crowd at the swill pen drew nearer, ears drinking every word, long parched for anything out of the ordinary. It reminded Myron of children watching a traveling magician transform scarves into live rats on the bed of a wagon, a spectacle Myron had witnessed as a kid on the road to Copper Creek.

Saul reached for Errol's hand, twisting it to show the tattoo on the back. "That's an Agriculture tattoo."

Errol pulled his hand back, giving it a rub. "Okay, so I got pretty good with mules." He pointed his finger at the crowd. "When the last of your machines fall apart, the mule tenders, well, let's just say I'll be on top for a change."

Myron glanced at Sindra again, who still would not look at him.

The textile woman approached the stranger. "I've been here in Jonesbridge since I was old enough to pull a lever," she said, her hair in a brown bun twisted tightly on top of her head. "Always dreamed of seeing someplace else, maybe with thatch-roofed houses and dogs barking, whistle of a teakettle calling me home. See anything like that out there?"

Errol laughed. "Best keep your dreams, then, because that's all they are. There's nothing out there worth seeing. Not one damn thing."

Like the woman, even though his six months couldn't compare to her thirty years, Myron had already lived in Jonesbridge too long, but unlike Errol, Myron knew there had to be *something* out there, something worth fighting for.

"Too much dying over nothing," the woman said, gazing through the swill pen as though she could see something other than an ochrous mountain behind a gray veil.

"All right, break it up," one of the nearby ghosts snapped, heading to the small group beside the one-legged man. "Due to recent events, curfew is in effect." He waved his jerry-rod through the crowd, striking slogs at random. "Get your ration and get to your room."

Myron and Sindra locked eyes. He cast his gaze toward the tunnel behind the domicile. Sindra's jaw bulged, her shoulders squared, and her eyes moved in Saul's direction. Myron turned toward the commissary slowly and got a look at Saul's face. He was staring right at Sindra.

"If you've got your ration, get going," a ghost snapped, prodding Saul with his discipline rod. Myron had already made his way to the commissary door. Saul kept glaring at Sindra and then at Myron.

"It's them," Saul yelled, walking backward toward the stairs. "I've seen them sneaking around. I'll bet they're the ones."

The four ghosts overseeing the commons glanced at the end of the ration line where Myron and Sindra stood and convened near the benches, where they spoke amongst themselves for several seconds, growing agitated. "You!" One of the ghosts called to Saul. "Come over here."

When Saul arrived, the head ghost whipped Saul's hand over and jotted down his tattoo number onto her clipboard. "You will be expected to report to salvage administration for questioning, first thing in the morning before your shift."

Sindra lined up behind Myron. "We have to get out of here," she whispered without moving her lips. "*Tonight.*"

The head ghost marched toward them. She held a finger above each head in line until she reached Myron. Saul nodded from across the commons. The ghost grabbed Myron's hand and added his tattoo number to the list before moving to Sindra.

"You," the ghost said to Myron, "report to salvage administration for questioning prior to your shift. And *you.*" She turned to Sindra tapping her clipboard, examining her through narrow eyes, looking her up and down. "Report to re-orientation for interrogation."

The skin around Sindra's eyes grew pale along with her lips, and her eyes welled with tears at the mere thought of a stint in the stretcher, but she kept her composure. It reminded Myron of seeing someone choke, unable to speak or breathe. He made sure he showed no emotion whatsoever, no pity, or shame, and swallowed his desire to take the blame immediately to keep Sindra out of a stretcher interrogation. Neither of them moved or breathed until the the ghost continued up the line, scrutinizing the hungry slogs who also held their breath and kept their eyes straight forward as she passed.

The line dwindled as each slog approached the counter where Millie cross-referenced tattoos with ration distribution, doling out protein and bread as appropriate, each ration costing exactly what the worker had made that day in wages. Sindra took her ration and headed for the door, again making brief, insistent eye contact with Myron, who waited at the counter, the last slog in line.

Millie frowned, scanning the ration book, checking under the counter and studying her cart. "I'm sorry, Myron." Her mouth hung open in disbelief as she checked the ration book a second time. "We—we're short today. We're never short. I'm sorry." She extended her empty hands toward Myron.

"Okay, commissary's closed." The two ghosts standing guard at the door approached Myron and ushered him into the swill pen.

He headed for the stairs, intermingling with other slogs in the group to keep inconspicuous. He had already timed the patrols at the rear of the courtyard, so he nudged Sindra in the direction of the grate behind the quad.

With the courtyard emptying for curfew, they had no time to go one ahead of the other like they did last time, so they slipped into the shadow of the stairs together and through the narrow space between the domicile buildings. Myron held up his hand for her to stop. When he reached thirty in his count, two ghosts meandered past in the opposite direction.

As they tiptoed in the direction of the tunnel, Myron's empty stomach threatened to heave. With the grate gone from last night's incident, and the dead ghost found next to the hole, someone had filled the hole completely with heavy stones. He should have assumed that, but his desire to get Sindra out of Jonesbridge had clouded his judgment.

"They've sealed the tunnel. There's no way in."

"No, no. My star."

"Keep track of our time. Count to thirty," Myron knelt down. Under the dim light from the domicile quad security lamp, he scratched out a map in the dirt. Sindra bent down beside him.

"Can't go now. Wait until the night shift break whistle. When ghosts do shift change, sneak out," he spoke as fast as he could as he drew in the dirt. "Follow the dark bank of the Yarin. Do not cross the bridge. Follow until you reach the salvage outtake. Cross through the water under the bridge."

Myron cast her a quick glance to quash her protest. "Twenty-one, Twenty-two," she whispered reminding Myron how much longer they had.

"Snake around to the furnace chute. Follow up along the opposite side wall to an old wooden grate like this one." Myron sped through the instructions. "Got it?"

Sindra nodded, her lips moving as she counted. "Twenty-eight," Sindra whispered.

Myron wiped his map clean, grabbed Sindra's hand and headed for the the domiciles.

Hunkered at the base of the stairs, Myron timed the guards in the swill pen. "I've never done what we're about to do. I don't know if it's possible. I don't even know where the other tunnel leads, if anywhere. But just in case something happens to me, at least you know how to get to the other grate," he whispered almost inaudibly, though he had doubts she would be able to find it without him based on the hurried directions he'd given her. Sindra pulled Myron's empty ration sack open and peered inside. Then she dropped in her protein stick with a smile. They looked at each other the remaining five seconds before heading their separate ways, slipping back into their proper rooms before bed check.

CHAPTER 6

Myron sat on his cot and stared at the spent coals in his stove, trying not to fall asleep. All day he had sensed an illness coming on with intermittent fever and chills. Three pieces of torn fabric draped across his knee. He pulled his needle, fashioned from a splinter of pine, through one piece of cloth and aligned the other so it overlapped. His hands shaking from the cold, wanting to save his last piece of coal, he pierced the other fabric, sewing the swatches together with as tight of a stitch as he could make.

The fabric was sheer and lightweight, women's undergarments that had been soiled or worn through and discarded in the burn heap to generate steam for mine trolleys. Women were afforded such luxuries as a matter of necessary hygiene given their regularities. His first attempt to handle these garments a few months ago made his stomach turn, but he could find no other material suitable. The burlap they wore on the factory floor was too porous, everything else, too heavy. After four hundred or so pairs and months of sewing, he finally got used to it.

So far, he had fashioned fourteen panels of fabric to make seven gores total of his airship balloon, completing the envelope with each one in the case he had to go quickly and had no time to sew. For thread he'd pulled apart discarded burlap strand by strand. Myron figured there would be leaks in the balloon, but if he got his fire hot enough, without setting the whole contraption ablaze, he banked that he could at least get across the Gorge. The last bit he held in his hand would comprise the deflation port at the top. Once attached, he would have his balloon, much smaller than he'd planned, but it might work. The other pieces—what made it a real airship instead of just a balloon—Myron admitted made his contraption look more like a pouncing insect with a coal pan for a thorax than an airship, but he had faith in the scientific principles he'd learned from his grandfather.

After he finished connecting the three swatches, Myron gathered a handful of metal nuts and bolts of various sizes, his ration of coal, and the hinged ceramic plate he smuggled out today. He pulled the loose bricks out behind his cot and retrieved the *Atlas of the Modern World* and *The Physics of Flight*, another ancient textbook from the Old Age that described great flying machines that floated on airfoils powered by turbine jets, something he could hardly imagine.

He cinched it all in the last piece of stitched fabric he would have for his airship and set it aside, waiting for the night shift break whistle to sound so he and Sindra could make their escape. Each time his head nodded, Myron perked up to keep awake, but his whole body had begun to ache. He tried pacing but his fatigue overcame him, so he sat on the edge of his cot, ears tuned to the distant whistle, his mind wandering.

Most slogs stuck in the Jonesbridge Industrial Complex had spent much longer there than Myron or Sindra. Some had toiled away nearly a lifetime and never knew or understood or remembered that life was more than sacrifice. Myron often wondered if his memories were real. They seemed so distant, as though they had to burrow through the wall of smoke and gray snow to find them. The memories of his grandfather were the clearest, their conversations and his advice. Myron treated these recollections as he did the rare pastries in his ration—afraid to consume them, as though he could relive the moment only once and then it would be gone, the way his grandfather told him a bee dies after it stings.

Myron had loved the books, the smell of leather and the crackle of flipping paper late at night, a candle flame so close it threatened to hop right onto the page there with his grandfather's gaze. His grandfather also loved kites, especially the boxy kind, kites as rectangular as Block 14-C. He and his grandfather flew them when the wind allowed. But Myron's grandfather used to say that a good bicycle could take a man to the ends of the earth and back, that he could pedal until the shackles dropped from his ankles and then go some more, the narrow wheels bobbing over rocks, sliding through ruts, chain muscling through the gears, that a man can feel the countryside he's crossing on a bicycle. Riding across a hilltop near Richterville, he could see his grandfather waving.

Myron's head bobbed and he realized he had fallen asleep. His heart raced as he hopped to his feet. He cracked the door open, thankful for the dark horizon. He wondered how long he had slept, minutes, hours, and he had no idea whether he should go now, or wait to see if the break whistle hadn't yet blown. Of all times to lose focus. Myron kicked his cot and rubbed his face.

He shook his canteen with his ration of fresh water, only half full. Inching the door open again, he stepped out to the corridor, checking both directions for patrols. With his bundle in hand, he shut the door behind him. The floor creaked as he made his way toward the stairs. Up against the wall, Myron peered around the corner to the swill pen, still angry that he didn't know whether he was early or late and whether Sindra had understood his directions, whether she would make it without him.

Ghosts changed shift midway between slog shifts so that any gap in coverage would go unnoticed because slogs would either be asleep or at work. Exactly when they underwent this change of guard remained a mystery to most, but Myron made so many trips out to the bunker where he stored his airship parts that he had memorized every movement of the ghosts on patrol. Each night after bed check, if he had something to add to his contraption, Myron sneaked to the chapel through the tunnel and followed the creek bed to a concrete bunker constructed in a long ago war where soldiers aimed through a slot and shot at their enemies. That's where he'd found his flashlight, something they wouldn't have tonight. Getting to the grate behind the domicile had been easy compared to what he was about to try.

Two ghosts rounded the corner below and entered the empty courtyard. They were not the same ghosts Myron had seen before bed check. He knew immediately that he had slept through the break whistle. They had already changed shifts, and Sindra was probably already out there somewhere along the route he had worked out, scared and wondering where he was.

Night shift lasted twelve hours. Ghosts changed over midway, giving him and Sindra six hours to get lost on the rim by the time day shift started. Myron pulled his arm short of punching the wall and darted to the stairs, praying they still had most of those six hours and that he could make it to the other grate unseen.

On each floor he hid in the shadow and waited for the spot light to pass, then took another flight of stairs. On the ground floor, the light came close to catching him, and he winced as though a flame had singed his hair. He hadn't explained the spotlight to Sindra. If the Great Above really did watch over people the way his grandfather claimed, maybe she would make it.

Myron felt like a field mouse as he zipped from wall to wall, through housing blocks he never got a look at, and though they were identical to his own, each block hid the mystery of the thoughts holed up inside them, a personality that reflected the shift and the job of each individual it housed. By the time he made it beyond 12-D, he could see the canal glistening under the dim lights of adjacent factories.

Access to the Yarin Canal from the salvage factory side would have made their escape much simpler, but at night the lights from the factories illuminated that bank, along with most of the water. The raised walkway on the opposite bank cast a narrow shadow, concealing a ledge about as wide as Myron's foot where the brick that formed the wall of the canal met with the substructure of the walkway above it, where the ghosts roamed on patrol. Myron shimmied down a signal pole to the ledge, alarmed that he was halfway to the other grate and had seen no sign of Sindra.

The coal barge that shuttled loads of coal from the trains to the factories passed with a low rumble as Myron tied his bundle to his waist and lined up inside the shadow of the walkway. He prepared himself for the trek down the canal, a waterway flanked on both sides by steep walls. A slip from the ledge he stood on would send him into the frigid water with no way to climb out.

Step after step he hugged the wall, almost losing his balance where the scum build up grew slippery. The humming of countless turbines vibrated in his ears. The smell of the canal watered his eyes as the wake from another barge sloshed up over his feet. Creeping along a wall covered in slime, he feared, would take more time than he had.

Boots of patrolling ghosts pounded above him along with harsh voices stolen by the wind. The ledge narrowed further until he had to turn his feet sideways. Then Myron shut his eyes, concentrated on the beach scene in Bora Bora, and worked toward the salvage factory inch by inch reminding himself that Sindra had been a rail-walker. She had honed the art of sneaking. She could make it.

When the Yarin took a turn and branched in two, Myron realized he had almost arrived. The narrower canal, drainage from the salvage factory, oozed with the smell of the sanitizer they used. Even at night, with only the reflection of the factory lights, the green luster of the water flickered. Here the steep walls on either bank tapered away to sloped earth. Myron stepped from the tiny ledge to the slope and lay back to catch his breath.

He had never seen the factory from the opposite bank. The way it rose from the water's edge, speckled with lights from windows that overlooked the salvage bay. Beneath the turbine hum and the muffled clanks of slogs at work, Myron heard what sounded like sniffling. He leapt to his feet, scanning the darkness under the bridge. He jogged toward the sound, heartened by it and dismayed at the same time.

"Sindra," he whispered. On the lighted bridge above him, three ghosts stood sentry. Myron hopped from shadow to shadow. "Sindra."

"Myron," her faint voice returned. "What happened? Where were you?"

Myron arrived to find Sindra inches away from the water with her knees pulled up to her chest. He held a finger to his mouth and pointed to the bridge directly above them, but the nearby turbines created such a racket that he figured no one could hear them whispering anyway.

"I thought you left without me. I tried to make it across, but—" Sindra pretended she hadn't been crying "—I can't swim, Myron. I thought I could, but I don't know how."

Myron put his arm around her and kneeled down. "How long have you been here?" He hoped to estimate how much time they had.

"I don't know."

"I'm sorry, Sindra." Myron held out his hand and lifted her up. "I can swim. I'll help you. We'll make it, but we have to stay under the bridge."

Myron dipped his foot into the canal. The freezing water shot chills all the way to the top of his head. "When the warm slurry hits the water, that's when we go."

After a few minutes, they heard a rush of liquid from

underneath the factory spill into the canal. From the outtakes it whirled into a spiral of chemical sludge. Myron waded in, motioning for Sindra. He stuck a leg in the water first and then both legs until he was in up to his waist. The icy water felt like a thousand pinpricks until the hot waste water mixed in. Myron worked his arm under Sindra and eased in all the way, now feeling as though he would pass out at any moment.

"We have to hurry." Under the cover of the bridge, he pushed off the sludge on the canal bed toward the other bank, his teeth chattering. He kicked his legs and pulled the water with his free arm. Based on the smell and the noxious slicks on the surface, he hoped he could keep both their heads from going under. Supporting Sindra while his body threatened to freeze into a motionless lump, he pulled the water, swimming as his grandfather had taught him until he felt the bottom with his toes. Afraid that the canal would swallow them both, Myron heaved Sindra in the direction of the opposite bank, and in doing so, he slipped, submerging his entire head under the muck.

Ahead of him, Sindra reached for his hands and dragged him out, where she fell onto the bank, rolling Myron up out of the water with her. Myron's chest heaved violently. He couldn't stop coughing.

"Myron." Sindra put her hand under his head.

He could taste chemical fumes on his tongue and feel the glop in his nose. He rolled to his stomach and vomited, still coughing. With one hand cupped over his mouth to muffle the sound, Myron crawled up the bank with Sindra still in the shadow of the bridge. The hacking continued, making his lungs feel as though something had shut a valve off in his chest.

"What was that?" Above them two ghosts leaned over the bridge. A beam of light crisscrossed just beyond Sindra's foot.

Myron clamped both hands over his mouth and concentrated on taking tiny breaths through his nose, but the noxious stink in his nostrils made his eyes water and his chest heave. His quieter coughing, now lost in the drone of the nearby factories, finally subsided. Behind them, a sliver of gray twilight rose on the horizon. Rather than six hours, they had less than one. "We have to get dry," Myron whispered. He struggled to his feet, light-headed from his coughing fit and feeling feverish. He led Sindra to a rectangular slot that vented the furnace fire for the factory. Inside, an orange fireball roiled over a bed of coal. They lay beneath the vent, Myron considering the real possibility that with the illness and the cold this night could be his last, and a warm current washed over him, engulfing him in wool and lace.

CHAPTER 7

"Wake up, Myron."

He rejoined the world with Sindra slapping his face.

"The sun's coming up."

Crawling first, he got to his feet and followed the wall as far as they could before reaching an open area they would have to cross to get to the opposite side of the salvage factory. Peach and gray hues had overtaken much of the eastern sky, but they still had cover of darkness. From a distance, all the factories and smelters blended into one, but up close, they differed in so many ways. The smells and sounds of tool and die and the machinists, the smelters, all worlds unto themselves with mechanisms, and in a matter of minutes, the bricked paths before them would fill with slogs and ghosts, one line heading to work, the others off to the domiciles blocks.

Flat up against the wall, Myron leaned out, saw four ghosts heading their way and motioned to Sindra. "We'll have to go around." In a half-squat, he jogged across the path to the Requisitions facility where slog foremen checked out specialty tools and supplies for their crews. He jumped over a short wall and lay flat underneath the line of sight from the window. Sindra followed. They slinked on their bellies like a couple of rock lizards to an acid slag drainage ditch for the iron smelter and followed it to the aqueduct that supplied water to the boilers. From there they circled behind the ghosts to the spot where Myron had seen the other grate.

This wooden grate resembled the one behind 14-C in every way. It was the same size and shape, and it had the same light rust color as the ground, almost unnoticeable. This tunnel had enticed Myron since the first time he saw it but the traffic and all the eyes near it made it inaccessible except during a shift.

"This is it. Ready?"

Myron caught Sindra staring off into the distant mountains on the other side of the Gorge. She nodded and he hoisted the grate open to reveal a dark hole with no visible bottom unlike the one they traveled through to the chapel. Almost a foot below the opening, a ladder led into complete darkness. The sky had lightened. The first shift whistle blew, fifteen minutes until the paths would fill.

He took a deep breath and climbed down behind Sindra, repositioning the grate overhead. Rung by rung they descended. The ladder creaked with each step, loosening in places with their weight. Above him, Myron watched the square of light shrink to the size of a ration token.

"Myron, the ladder ends." Sindra's voice trembled.

"Do you see the bottom? Can you step down?" Myron

twisted, craning his neck for a view around Sindra.

"No. And there's nothing below."

Once when he and his grandfather had come upon an abandoned well, his grandfather had dropped a rock and counted until he heard the splash to estimate the depth. From his bundle of supplies, Myron pulled out a nut he planned to use on his airship. "Listen." He held his hand out straight and dropped the nut. A plop sounded somewhere between the counts of three and four.

"I'll go first." Myron climbed down behind Sindra on the ladder. "Once we drop, there's no going back. If this tunnel dead ends—"

"Yeah, I know."

Myron counted to three and pushed off the ladder, bracing for the hard impact with the ground. Moments later, he landed in a mushy soup of earth where he sank all the way to his knees. He couldn't see anything, but he could hear a faint trickle of water.

"Are you okay?"

"Farther than I thought. It's a mess. Like quicksand." He tugged at his legs mired in mud that made a sucking sound when he jerked his foot out.

"Quicksand? Hang on, I'm coming."

"Wait. If this doesn't go anywhere, you can climb back out."

The pinpoint of sky above him gave just enough light for Myron to see the old red brickwork under a wet film of soot and mud. Each step took its toll on his energy, freeing one leg, only for the other to sink down again. He worked in the direction of darkness until he met a wall of rubble. He walked his fingers across the edges of the stones in a panic, lamenting the justice of escaping one prison right into another one.

"Myron."

The damp walls of stone and muck muffled Sindra's voice. When his hand located a void in the stone, he slithered through to a crawlway and out again. "Come on. I think there's an opening."

Sindra plopped into the mire behind him where Myron extended his hand and pulled her toward him into complete darkness. "I can't see a thing. I'm scared, Myron."

"Me too," he whispered.

Each step forward required Myron and Sindra to grope for openings in the crumbling rock, as this pitch black tunnel snaked more than the one to the chapel. Every dead end stopped Myron's heart until he finally located another way through. "Looks like we're going to have to crawl."

"I hate this. Closed in spaces. It's so dark." Sindra let out a shriek and slapped at the rocks, hitting Myron on the nape instead.

"Let's take a break." Myron squinted, squeezed his eyes shut, and then held them open, hoping he would see something: Sindra, a stone, the ground, anything, but he only stared into the void. The mud had grown shallow as they moved farther into the tunnel, the walls more sloped, giving them a place to get off their feet. Sindra sat close beside Myron where they hugged each other for warmth.

"Somewhere up there, they're looking for us by now."

"Yeah." Myron shivered. His chills and fever had worsened rapidly. He imagined the admonition the superintendent would deliver this morning: *Two slogs wanted for questioning in the murder of a dutiful civil guard, not only shirked their duty but fled in what can only be taken as an admission of guilt.*

"You don't—think differently about me, do you?"

"What do you mean?" Though Myron suspected what she meant.

"Last night. What happened with the guard."

"Oh." Myron had tried to forget what he'd seen, Sindra being ravaged by that ghost. He couldn't imagine such a thing, a man forcing himself on a woman in a physical way. Though he knew that the animal inside him had been trapped and caged long ago—from the first day he arrived at the Jonesbridge Smokeworks to *focus on the progress of industry for the greater good*—Myron still thought about physical pleasure. It was intended for two people to share, not for one to steal from another. "Just sorry that had to happen."

"Bug and a few others tried to get on with me sometimes when I slept on the rail, but I could fight off the rail-walkers. Here—I can't." Sindra hugged Myron tighter. "The ghosts come in the middle of the night. Sometimes they don't even wake me up first. I'm just a carpie to them. They give me extra rations to keep me *thick*."

"That's terrible."

"And you know that all girls get sterilized in Jonesbridge. That's the first thing they do."

As far as Myron knew, what they explained during orientation, was that child birth and child rearing were delicate procedures best left to qualified people. Such activities disrupted production and caused distractions within the population. Civility raised and educated children to ensure the safety of future generations. But none of it ever made any sense to Myron. Industry needed more workers. Defense needed more soldiers. Women should have babies all the time, slogs, ghosts, Ag, whoever, babies everywhere to fill the gaps. The way they operated now, soon there would be no one left.

Sindra leaned her head on Myron's shoulder. "The thing is, I don't think the procedure worked on me," She finally said.

"What do you mean?"

"A girl just knows these things, Myron. Women have regularities, even barren women have them, or they can, but when they stop…" She rubbed her face. "There are other changes, too. But that doesn't matter. I think I'm pregnant."

"How'd you keep it from Doc?" Myron did know that if Doc ever discovered her condition, he would do the sterilization procedure again, better this time.

"That hack has such a loose fitting he wouldn't know the difference between a baby and limestone block."

Myron hadn't seen Doc since the last time he purpled a toe to the frost. Doc had given him a mouthful of billet thistle and a leather strap to bite down on, and then he'd snipped the toe off with a pair of red-hot snips.

"I'm glad though. Not that all that other stuff happened, but to know I can still bear a child. I want to keep my womanhood, Myron, and no one can ever find out that I have."

Myron and Sindra pulled as close to each other as possible and, leaning against the damp wall, fell into a shivering sleep. Myron dreamt of giant winged creatures swooping down to bite the heads off of everyone in Jonesbridge. They carried them to a nest high on Patriots Pass and recycled them into useful weapons. With his fever fueling one fitful dream after another, he awoke suddenly to a whooshing sound. His eyes popped open to blackness.

"Sindra. Wake up!" he shook her shoulder. Water began to rise in the tunnel, flowing from the direction they had come.

"What's happening?"

"I don't know. Drainage?" The water level reached their knees, continuing a slow rise to their waists and then chests. They lifted off the ground treading, rising with the water until Myron's head struck the top of the tunnel. "Stay up."

"It smells so bad. I can't breathe."

"Brimstone." Myron coughed, now unable to stand. "Munitions plant." He treaded water, keeping his mouth and nose as close to the top as possible.

"I don't want to drown." Sindra gasped for air as Myron helped her stay above the waterline, pulling her to a spot where the ceiling had a recess, until a current tugged at Myron's feet, pulling him downward toward the crawlway he'd discovered earlier. The water began to recede slowly at first until it drained completely as fast as it had risen. Myron and Sindra collapsed in the mud. "At least we now know this tunnel leads somewhere."

Myron's body aches extended all the way from the tip of his head to his toes. He would have sat there motionless and stared into blackness if not for the adrenaline that fueled his effort down the throat of the tunnel, wiggling around jagged rocks and over mounds of bricks and mud, hoping to beat the next rush of water. Sindra crawled behind him, never lagging out of reach of Myron's foot.

Slithering through the crawlways like a snake along a trail of sulfur mud and only the Great Above knew what else, Myron was glad for the first time that he couldn't see anything. Seeing the glop he pressed his hands into or the muck that dripped on his head, seeing how small the space really was might have frightened him more than going in blind. He found it easier to focus on one inch at a time rather than imagine how far it was to Bora Bora.

Myron couldn't tell how long they crawled, it felt like an hour, but he eventually reached an opening and managed to sit up without hitting his head on the ceiling. He stretched his arms and legs, and let out a sigh of relief when the outline of Sindra's face materialized. "Light." He pointed behind her.

Sindra helped Myron to his feet. She slung his arm over her shoulder and they tramped down a pipe toward a growing circle of light at the end. If he had focused on all of the possibilities, he would've lost his courage, but now that they'd made it through, all those potential problems bombarded him at once. Where would they come out, he wondered—and dreaded. Hopefully they would step out somewhere near Iron's Knob, maybe even close to the chapel or the bunker, anywhere as long as it was outside the compound perimeter. He even considered, with the rushing water, they might have gone all the way to the Gorge itself. Regardless of where they emerged, there was no returning the way they had come.

Myron shielded his face. Even the subdued light from a dull sky shrouded in smoke stung his eyes when they reached the opening.

"What is that?" Sindra braced herself and took a peek outside the mouth of the pipe.

Myron joined her. A stream of water still trickled from the pipe into a canal that spilled directly into the Great Gorge only two hects away. "That's the bridge. The one and only way across the Gorge." Everyone arrived in Jonesbridge either blindfolded or in a windowless train car. Myron had never seen the bridge this close with all the detail that his imagination had supplied.

The width of the crossing accommodated four ground transports abreast, and Myron also counted four rail tracks. The length of the famous suspension bridge, what his grandfather had touted as an engineering marvel first begun during the dying years of the Old Age some two hundred years ago, stretched as far as Myron could see and disappeared into haze and smoke. From their vantage point, he could make out two suspension towers and so many cables they formed a spider web in the sky.

"We have a problem." Myron studied the horizon in all directions.

"What?"

"That Gorge is even bigger than I thought." Myron was unsure if he had squirreled away enough coal to fuel his airship that far. He had planned for a rapid ascent into the cloak of a smoke bank and then a descent gradual enough to sail them to the opposite side of the gorge.

"I can't even see the other side."

"There's that—and there're ghosts all over the place. Defense, too. And train guards. Artillery." Myron slapped his hand on his forehead. He'd always known they would have no chance to get across the bridge, or through the Gorge, but seeing it, he never imagined such a bustling hub of activity. He counted two trains parked in the depot, dozens of train crew offloading crates onto mule drawn carts.

"Wow."

"There's the perimeter fence. Looks like we're outside the compound." Myron craned his head behind them, seeing a sheer rock face, the same as on either side of the pipe. "Keep down," he whispered and stepped out onto the wall of the canal edging along in the opposite direction of all of the activity. The first place he found to leave the canal bank, Myron cut through a few shin pines and hid behind a boulder. The fence, crisscrossed with wire and sharpened points of wood, rose in front of him and stretched from the bridge to the horizon.

"Look." Myron pointed to a supply train unloading crates, all labeled *Level 3 Rations-D1* and emblazoned with the same curious red biohazard rings around the circle that the ceramic-hinged plate had.

"Ration crates." Sindra's eyes widened. "I'm so hungry."

"Me too." Myron imagined that a pregnant woman might need to eat more often than everyone else. He figured that maybe one of their problems had been solved if they could make off with enough food to survive until they made their flight over the Gorge.

When the train crew finished unloading the ration crates, a heavy gate swung open over the rail tracks for the train to pull out of the depot, leaving the crates unguarded. The slow moving train had to first make a turn through the roundhouse and out of the compound, which would allow them just enough time to pilfer extra rations.

"Wait here. No reason to risk both of us going."

"Let me do it. If it's one thing I'm good at, it's swiping stuff," Sindra said.

Myron nodded. "Don't get greedy."

"I know. Just what we can carry."

"I don't see any guards now, but keep an eye on me," Myron insisted. "I'll signal you if someone is coming, and you get out of there."

"Okay." Sindra darted to the large pole that hinged the gate and skirted around it, keeping low and waiting for her opportunity.

Myron had lost strength. They needed to eat, but he knew this was risky. A rush of excitement ran through him. Since the day he arrived in Jonesbridge, he had planned for this day, all the preparation, smuggling supplies to the rim, dreaming of the crystal blue sky as he rose above the haze in his airship, and once they trekked to the secret bunker, the time would finally come.

He watched Sindra, crouched by the fence as though she might pounce. After he lost his mother and grandfather, Myron had convinced himself that no person would ever mean more to him than his own survival until he met Sindra, but everything meant more to him now. Risks seemed greater than they once did, now that he had someone to lose.

When the depot platform cleared of workers, Sindra slipped through the gate. Myron held his breath. He heard a noise behind him. Blood rushed from his head trying to figure out what made the noise. He turned around suddenly to a human wall of fur. A moment later everything went black.

CHAPTER 8

On all fours, Sindra crept through the gate and edged along the berm of gravel that supported the railroad tracks. The twin rails bore the weathered patina of black iron on the sides, and on top, the wheels of moving trains had burnished the metal to a silvery sheen. Even the smell of the creosote timbers reminded her of the free life walking the rails.

Sindra stared along tracks as they disappeared into a wall of haze on the bridge, a living rail that actually led to a destination where workers loaded and unloaded supplies. The other end of the line drew her as though she could stroll up the tracks, hopping from one timber to the next until she reached a quaint village nestled in a sunny meadow.

In the territories to the South, where Sindra's clan of rail-walkers wandered, the rails they traveled often ended in blown-out bridges, collapsed tunnels, dead ends where the track simply stopped, destroyed many wars ago. With the rails cut off, without the trains, bits of civilization withered away the way a toe purpled from frost bite. First a toe, then a foot and a leg, then two; towns grew smaller and farther apart, until only their carcases remained.

Voices and footsteps sounded from beyond the crates. Sindra searched for Myron on the other side of the fence, for an all-clear signal, but she couldn't spot him anywhere. The perimeter fence, a structure she had never seen with clarity until today, rose to the height of three people stacked foot to head. At a distance, winding through the haze at the base of the hills, it looked like a solid structure. Up close, she could see it for what it was, precarious and uninviting, and anything but solid, composed of metal lattice tangled with razor wire, easy to see through, difficult to penetrate, especially with spikes jutting out from the ground on either side spanned by more tight rolls of razor wire.

As they always did when she was afraid, the tips of her fingers tingled as she wedged between two columns of crates stacked five high, wondering what happened to Myron, if she should run back now or stay for the food. Old Nickel once told her on the rails that survivors seized opportunities, casualties shied away from them, and this opportunity had presented itself as if by providence. They had emerged from the tunnel at the supply depot. The gate was open. Ration crates lined up for the taking, and with the life inside her demanding more, hunger had taken the reins of her judgment.

Sandwiched between the crates, she noticed that not all of them were the same. Though she couldn't read the words, the symbols differed. One set of crates displayed a green square underneath the writing, and the other set, emblazoned with a red circle and three partial red circles coming out from the center, caught her eye.

Too bulky to carry, she'd have to open one of the boxes and take what she could stuff into her smock. When the train behind her released its steam with a whoosh, smothering any noise she might make, Sindra punched a hole in the nearest carton with her thumb and peeled the top back. Inside, dozens of beige protein sticks lay side by side under butcher paper wrap. She grabbed one and bit off the end, chewing, swallowing and biting again to quash the rumble in her stomach.

Sindra had possessed a weakness for food even before she got pregnant. It was how she acquired her rail-walker name, Pumpkin Stew. She had run with the clan for nearly three months before they finally bestowed her with a name. All rail-walkers got their names the same way, from something that stood out about them, some little detail that caught on. Old Nickel earned hers from the coin pendent she wore around her neck, said it was an ancient currency from before the Great Zeolot War. They called Sindra Pumpkin Stew because she was first in line for pumpkin stew and first to come around again to scrape the bottom of the pot.

How she wished she could dig into a bowl of turnip and pumpkin stew at that very moment. Those protein sticks tasted the same way they looked, gray and dry with an after hint of sour rye, a flavor she had not yet grown accustomed to her entire time in Jonesbridge.

"Looks like we're light on Civility rations again. Go ahead and get this other lot to the slog ration station." A voice on the other side of the crates said.

Sindra froze. She scanned the brush where she and Myron had squatted earlier. She couldn't spot him anywhere.

No signs of him, no movement, nothing. He wasn't there. Her breathing quickened. Even in the frosty breeze, a sweat broke out on her forehead.

"What's the difference? Just give 'em some of the slogs' ration." Another voice said. Sindra held her breath and remained like a statue.

"We can't do that."

"It's good enough for us, ought to be good enough for them."

"I don't make the rules. Blue square, Civility. Red circles—Industry," the voice said.

The shadow covering Sindra shrank suddenly. Above her, two crates disappeared, moments later, two more. She hunkered lower, rolling herself into a ball, still scanning for signs of Myron. He should have warned her somehow, given her signal to get out of there.

Fingers wrapped around the box closest to her head. Sindra gathered as many protein sticks as she could and shoved the rest over on the loading dock. As the boxes tumbled into the shins of the two men, she bolted for the gate.

"What was that?"

"Thief!"

The gate had already begun to shut as Sindra arrived. Behind her, the shuffle of footsteps gained ground. She turned sideways and slipped through the closing gate, sliding her arm through first, then wiggling her body through the narrowing space, preparing to run as fast into the hills as she could. As she pulled with all her strength, a pair of hands around her arm yanked her back, and the gate began to open again. She tugged, wrenching her captor's hands around the gate pole and broke free before the gate swung open enough for the team of ghosts to get through.

"Stop!"

They gave chase. Sindra weaved through shin pines, staying ahead of them until dull pain struck her ankles. A discipline rod thrown from behind tripped her into the brambles, scattering her cache of protein sticks across a patch of gray snow. She landed face down.

Ghosts on either side of her hoisted Sindra to her feet. "What do we have here?" a ghost asked. He twisted Sindra's hand over to look at her tattoo. "Slog—shirker, thief." He tied Sindra's hands behind her behind her back.

"Come on." A ghost nudged her with a discipline rod, pushing her toward the gate.

She twisted around for one last look at the empty spot where Myron should have been, hoping for a glimpse of him, moving brush, a flicker of flesh darting into the shadows, but she saw no signs of him.

"Careful, this one's a biter," one of the ghosts remarked before he gave Sindra another push to keep her going. They passed through the gate and beyond the platform where the ration crates once stood. "Take her to Industry Admin."

Every step Sindra took in the direction of Jonesbridge erased a hard-fought step she and Myron had taken in the other direction. Her stomach growled and her legs ached, and she had no more energy to put up a fight. The closer she got to the Jonesbridge compound, the more those dreams she shared with Myron faded until they washed away in the shadows of the smokestacks. Myron could travel lighter now without her to weigh him down.

As was the custom when a slog shirked duty, other slogs

were notified who it was that had not pulled their weight.
"Shirker!" The ghost to Sindra's right shouted as they walked
through Jonesbridge. "Shirker!" He acted as a town crier
with news, and the slogs filed from their factories hearing
him shout.

Her hands bound behind her back, the ghost platoon
paraded Sindra, the apprehended shirker, down the brick
paths of Jonesbridge though hundreds of her fellow slogs.
Some jeered, others spat, but many kept their heads down,
refusing to look at her. The spectacle continued through
familiar sectors of Jonesbridge, the down run of the Yarin
Canal, green with yellow streaks by the time it reached the
salvage factory, Tool and Die, ore, the coal yards, but her
shame continued beyond the baths and the orientation block,
further than Copper, Iron, Munitions, and Assembly to the
Administration sector where the admins dwelled in domiciles
with water basins for cleaning and panes of glass on the
windows to keep out the wind and choking clouds of sulfur.
She arrived at last to the place where the Superintendent
wielded his authority, where his communications originated,
and where he cast the die for the their future.

The Industry Administration building resembled an
ornate, imposing factory on the outside with high walls
and soot-stained brick. Intricate gargoyles of workers with
bulging muscles dutifully guarded the façade over a frieze
etched with scenes from the construction of Jonesbridge
and the digging of the Great Gorge. Sindra labored up
the twenty-seven steps to the entrance, to the two doors
that rose to a height of a four story domicile quad. Two
limestone statues flanked the doors, on one side, a man
mining with a pickaxe, and on the other, a woman fastening

a rivet to a beam.

One look at the high vaulted ceiling as she stepped through the doors made Sindra feel as though her stomach might turn. Three tapestries draped the wall opposite the entrance, making them the first thing anyone would see. The largest showed the mustachioed Superintendent of Industry wielding a sledge hammer. Beside it, a woman with a flowing mane of auburn hair held a sickle in mid-swath over a golden pasture of wheat. The other one depicted a man with a rifle and a pair of binoculars surveying a battlefield from the edge of a precipice.

The sounds of her footsteps echoed across the expansive hall as the two ghosts escorted Sindra to a booth in the far corner of the room.

"Industry Colleague R231-B," a woman behind the desk called. She wore thick glasses and also used a magnifying lens to read the scribble in the journal. Her chair creaked as she twisted back and forth, shuffling papers. "Step forward."

Sindra limped into a square yellow box painted on the floor, holding out her hand for the clerk to verify her identity by her tattoo. Sindra's ribs still screamed every time she moved from the blows she'd sustained during her capture. Even though she stood only an arm's length from the administration clerk, the woman behind the desk still squinted, needing heavy lenses to see her.

"Full day's shirk." She positioned her magnifier on another open journal. "Compound breach. Ration theft," she muttered. "Resisting authorities." She clicked her tongue several times. "And, all on a day when you were expected for interrogation in the murder of a civil guard, which in my estimation makes you an accomplice." The woman shuffled through a stack of papers. "My, my, this is bad."

"But I—"

The clerk held up her hand. "Don't make it worse."

Sindra stifled her tears until they began to seep out. She squeezed her eyes shut, trying to maintain composure as she anticipated the punishment the clerk had in store for her.

The clerk pointed a pencil at Sindra. "There's a reason for our rules." She leaned across the desk and slapped her hand down. Her eyes looked like giant horsefly eyes behind her lenses. "Fifty people to feed. But only one piece of bread. Fifty fireboxes to fuel with only one piece of coal." She paused, staring straight into Sindra's eyes. "Fifty enemy soldiers to shoot. Only one bullet." She perused her papers. "It all works together. Do your duty to win the war."

Sindra nodded, unsure whether she had permission to speak.

After a lengthy silence the clerk pronounced the sentence. "Trial by stockade, three—no, four days in the shirker coop." She removed her thick lenses and looked up at Sindra with a stern but sympathetic glare. "And, *if* you survive your tribulation, you will undergo reorientation." The clerk tinged a bell on her desk.

Hearing her punishment made Sindra's knees weak. The world began to spin. She knelt down on all fours and threw up on the stone floor of the Industry Administration. The bile burned her dry throat.

A nearby ghost threw a burlap rag that landed on Sindra's neck. "Get that cleaned up."

She reached for the rag and dabbed the spot on the floor, and then wiped the drool from her mouth.

Two ghosts prodded her to her feet. "Come on."

The team of ghosts led Sindra down the main thoroughfare of the Industrial complex where overloaders laden with coal loaded barges, and slogs of all stripes convened en route to mines and factories. In the center of the common area between the machine shop and skilled munitions assembly, a ghost marched to a chain and lowered a cage that hung from an extended pulley. He yanked the door open and escorted Sindra into the cage, the shirker stockade. He affixed the shirker sign on the edge of the cage, and two of them pulled the chain until the middle of the enclosure lifted to eye level of passing slogs.

The trial by stockade was reserved for a slog suspected of shirking or any other capital crime thought to impede production. The *coop* was a cage too short to fully stand in and too narrow to lie down. The rules of the shirker coop dictated that a displayed slog may only have to drink and eat what other slogs offered from their own ration. If anyone felt enough sympathy to share from their own already paltry ration, the shirker might get enough water and food to survive the stint. The regular slog water ration barely kept a normal slog alive.

The only person Sindra had seen in the coop hadn't survived the ordeal, which implied a guilty verdict in the trial by peers. Since Sindra hadn't lived in Jonesbridge long, other than Myron, she doubted whether anyone would take enough pity on her to share. Without Myron, she lost hope.

Countless eyes of fellow slogs cut her angry glances as they passed. Some looked away, others paid no attention to her at all. The shift change completed and the streets emptied. Darkness fell and with it, the temperature. She hugged her ribs and squatted for warmth, working her tongue from cheek to cheek, trying to produce moisture to quench her thirst. The guards who raped her had given her extra rations in the past. No one wanted a carpie with axe blades for hips, they'd told her, but where were they now with their rations? Sindra grabbed the bars on the cage and rocked it, screaming. The factory noise smothered her clamor as though it had wrapped her pleas in a blanket and thrown them into the canal.

Every time she nodded to sleep, her shivering woke her, so she stared into the darkness where the yellow sparkles of factory lights dotted the landscape, dreaming that Myron would appear with a loaf and a sip of water. Tonight, Sindra faced a bitter, violent wind, a wind that acted to clear the air much more than usual. She took a breath, clean and cold, so cold she almost preferred the stink of smoke. She began to see shapes in the darkness, outlines of railroad tracks and Old Nickel's face standing next to Bug and Nap.

Shadows hopping from one place to the next, Sindra reached out to catch one. She heard a voice, unsure whether it was real, until she felt the warmth of a threadbare blanket slip through the bars on the cage.

"Here." The voice said. "Half my water." He passed a canteen through.

Sindra wrapped up in the blanket and squinted into the night to see who had shown so much kindness. Beside the cage, the new guy, the one-legged-man who had created quite a stir in 14-C recently with tall tales of the outside world. He leaned on his cane and spoke softly.

"I'll share what rations I can with you. May not be enough water to survive four days out here, though." He dug a dried sprig out of his smock. "Here. Chew on this barber weed. Something I give the mules from time to time to settle them down after an injury. It'll help you through the night. Might make you see strange things though."

"Thanks," Sindra whispered, pulling the blanket tighter. "Why are you helping me?"

"You and Myron are the only ones that know the way out of this place. Someday I'll expect you to show me the secret. You gotta survive this first."

"Myron's gone," she whispered, torn between her hope that he disappeared because he'd fallen in a hole or passed out from illness, and dreaming that he ran to his flying machine and sailed it over the Gorge.

He seemed not hear her, or not to care. "Besides," he went on, "I used to work as a mule man in a traveling preacherman show, thirty years back. Preacherman claimed that kind deeds sometimes come back around."

She watched as Errol hop-skipped on his crutch until his darkened body blended with the night. Sindra closed her eyes and imagined Myron's postcard with a picture of sunshine and warm sandy beaches.

CHAPTER 9

"Sindra!" Myron stumbled to his feet. Blood rushed from his head, and he fell backwards. His eyes came clear finally on the now familiar form of Coyote Man, leaning with his arms over his knees against the opposite wall.

"There you are. Not sure if you'd croaked on me or not," Coyote Man stated.

Myron backed away. Still woozy from his illness, his thoughts a kaleidoscope of dark tunnels and caves and plans gone wrong, Myron lunged at Coyote Man, leading with his fist. He threw a weak punch while flashes of the last thing he remembered, Coyote Man raising a board over his head as Myron waited for Sindra, drove him to strike again. He connected a blow just under Coyote Man's chin and followed with his left hand. He pounded on Coyote Man's chest, visions of Sindra, now out there alone, driving every blow.

Coyote Man did not budge, as though Myron had struck

a brick wall covered in fur. "Save your energy, boy. You've been pretty sick. Burning with the fever and shaking, talking the talk of a dying man."

Myron stopped to catch his breath as Coyote Man turned around and ducked underneath a ledge. Myron followed, limping out of a stone recess into a tiny cavern with a fire at its center, smoke billowing through a fissure topped with a narrow strip of sky. Hanging from an iron rod over the center of the fire was a rusted pot full of churning soup with chunks of brown and gray bobbing through the bubbles.

Coyote Man dipped a wooden scoop into the pot and handed it to Myron. "Bone stew," he said. "I call it coyote casserole." He filled a bowl for himself.

Steam rose from the scoop. Myron put the stew to his mouth. The hot liquid seeped into the cracks in his lips, giving them a sting.

Myron rubbed his head, still aching from Coyote Man thumping it with a log. "Why did you bring me here?"

"'Cause you and me are sailing out of here on that contraption of yours." Coyote Man pointed at Myron. "The sooner the better."

Myron spied his bundle containing his nuts and bolts and books and postcard of Bora Bora laying on a rock beside the fire, relieved that Coyote Man hadn't left it behind. "I'm not going anywhere without Sindra." Myron wobbled to his feet. Crawlways on both sides of the cavern wound into darkness, making his chance of picking the right one precarious.

"Your girly got sent back to Jonesbridge. Best forget about her." All beard and fur, Coyote Man scooped another bowl of stew with no concept of the betrayal he had set in motion, forcing Myron to abandon Sindra without a word.

"Rest. You'll need your strength."

Myron grabbed his bundle and darted into the closest passageway.

"Nothing you can do for her now!" Coyote Man called. "Best you get back in here and finish eating. We've got a gorge to cross." He chuckled. "Only one way out of here, and that ain't it."

Myron worked his way back into the open cavern, glaring at Coyote Man who sipped his stew without a care. Still weak, Myron walked past the fire and crawled into the other passage.

"That ain't it either."

Myron returned to the fire and found his bowl. Scooping another helping of bone stew, he situated himself on the other side of the pot. His surroundings came into focus gradually, his thoughts still blurry.

As he became more aware, he had a good look at the cavern, its formations and nooks and crannies, and for the first time, its beauty struck him. The moistened colors danced on the walls with the light of the flames, concealing countless recesses and corridors of minerals. Ponds of water filled low areas and echoed with drips from the ceiling where the ground above them sifted melted snow. Beside the fire, a group of stalagmites jutted up from the ground. Striated with limestone and calcium, they also bore the yellow tint of sulfur ribboned with silvery-white magnesium bands. Above them, the stalactites reached for their partners on the ground striving to one day form a single column. Myron recalled a legend that these two formations were the souls of lost lovers who pined away for each other until they finally joined into one.

The lip of Coyote Man's bowl disappeared into his beard as he finished off his stew. Myron followed suit, downing the rest of his meal, chomping the hunks of wild onions and sinew, gulping every morsel. He wiped the drops from his mouth.

"A mite better than the ground chaff and pig's tail ration they feed you in that compound. Coyotes won't even give that a sniff and they'll eat damned near anything. They'll eat the rations they give to the guards though, that's for sure. "

"I'm going back for Sindra."

"Hold your leathers, boy. You and me are flying that contraption out of here. Your girl is with them. No getting her back now."

Myron had feared that very thing, but hearing Coyote Man say the words aloud cemented it, no getting her back. "I am getting her back. I won't go without her."

Coyote Man's shadow climbed the glistening stone wall as he stood. "Three is too risky. Three can't keep a secret. Three can't be trusted. And three can't ride that tiny contraption."

"That's right! *You* are the third. If Sindra doesn't go, you don't go."

Coyote Man's eyes narrowed. "I know where you squirreled away all those supplies. Run off to Jonesbridge for that girl on a suicide mission and I might spread it all to kingdom come. If that contraption ever takes flight, it will be with me on board."

Coyote Man was right about one thing, three full-grown adults on an airship built for one—Myron didn't like the outcome of that equation, especially now that he'd seen the distance across the Gorge first hand. He would just have to string this wild man along, at least long enough to get in position to make the flight. "We don't go without Sindra. Either wait for me to help her out of there or turn my balloon to garbage, it won't matter, you'll still be stuck here in this cave—same as you were yesterday. Help me get Sindra, and we sail to freedom."

"You're a fool, boy, traipsing off on some trifling errand back into the mouth of hell. You escaped once. Now you want to return?"

"That's right."

"Look, this place is trickier than you might know. There are secrets woven into its walls, like dye into cloth."

"I know plenty."

"I can't make it over the gorge without you. And you can't make it out of here without me. You'll run out of untainted water, first thing. Drink that acid snow runoff and choke on your own spit."

Conceding that one argument to Coyote Man, Myron had thought of everything, except what he would do when his canteen ran dry. "Fine. But we need Sindra, too."

"What do we need her for?"

"Here, you've got the run of the place, with water and stuff. Sindra, she was a rail-walker. She knows how to find things out there, where all the leftover towns are. May not be any coyotes where we're going. May not be anything." Myron stood up. "So, if we're going to make it, I have to get Sindra. *Now*. Before it's too late."

Coyote Man paced around the fire, staring up at the rock ceiling just above his face. He reached for a stick wrapped in oil-soaked burlap and stuck it into the fire. "Not without a plan, you won't." He led Myron to a wall in the cavern and illuminated an intricate map drawn with chalk. "Here it is. This whole God-forgotten place from the bridge all the way back around. Didn't map inside the compound. Don't need it. Won't set foot in that place."

Myron thought Coyote Man had a peculiar way of speaking that made him wish he were sitting around the fire with his grandfather, learning new things, talking about airfoils and grand machines and ocean animals the size of houses. "Who are you, anyway? Where did you come from?"

After a moment, Coyote Man responded with a grunt. "Name's Ramani," he said with a nod. "Miner. Worked nights nearly thirty years. But that man died when I became a coyote. Call me whatever you want to."

Myron vaguely recalled a man that went missing a while back, a victim of the elements, who had dropped dead of the wet lung on his way to his shift. Ramani's beard blanketed his entire neck, but when Myron eyed his hands, he saw no tattoos of Industry, or of any other administration. "What happened to your tattoos?"

"They took me for a dead man. Didn't so much as look me over. Just tossed me in the bury-hole with three other folks that actually were croaked. Not much of a way to treat a fellow countryman, is it?" Ramani spat. "I woke up to a coyote licking my face. My tattoos? I scraped 'em off with piece of flint. Practically peeled my skin right off."

Myron studied the map as Ramani passed the torch along the wall. He had drawn every detail of the area bound by the Gorge, except for the inside of the compound. With his finger not quite touching the wall, Myron traced dry creek bed from the Gorge all the way to Iron's Knob and stopped at the old chapel, trying to get an idea of how far

Ramani's cave was from the places Myron knew.

"Don't plan on getting back in the way you got out. They cordoned off that area. Talking about a fugitive." He chuckled. "That must be you."

Myron knew he couldn't have gone that way, anyway. They had dropped at least fifteen feet from the ladder when they first went down into the drainage tunnel. There was no way up the other direction.

Coyote Man pointed his finger into Myron's chest with a thump. "Hear me, boy. All these mines and factories—they're desperately important, and they'll do whatever they have to do to keep unwanted people out and wanted people in. This place is secret. *Nobody* gets out of here. Not without a plan and a whole shitpot of luck. I know. I've tried."

"You've tried?"

"Many times. Got as far as a quarter of the way down that gorge with tackle and ropes and such. Thought I might choke. Too treacherous. Too deep. And I thought about just jumping off into the gorge a time or two—end it all right there." He stared at a point on the map. "Then there's trip wires, razor wire, armed guards, watchtowers. You name it. I've been patient here alone. Until I saw that contraption of yours start coming together. Patience has run out. I'm getting out of here, too."

Myron followed Coyote Man to an alcove under a calcite deposit that resembled glistening peeled potatoes. Beside Coyote Man's makeshift bed, Myron saw a set of shelves fashioned from crates that held a variety of supplies. "Here." Coyote Man handed Myron a water skin.

"What's that?" Myron pointed to a brown box similar to the speaker on the factory floor, except this one had a hand crank, like the one Myron used for light when he read his books.

Coyote Man reached for the box and pulled out a thin metal rod that had been concealed inside it as if folded in on itself from the inside.

"An antenna?"

"A radio. Made it myself. Well, most of it." Coyote Man turned the crank, slowly at first, then as the whine of gears smoothed, he cranked faster. "Just garbled static down here in the cave." He pressed his ear next to the speaker. "Topside, sometimes it's more than static." Coyote Man collapsed the antenna. "I swear that I've heard voices from out there. Singing."

Myron once heard that if the wind could carry the voices of the lost generations we would never know it because we didn't listen. He couldn't imagine the box capturing singing from somewhere out there, how wondrous a thought, but Myron figured Coyote Man had grown mad in his solitude.

"Clean water," Ramani yelled from another alcove. "There's the rub in this hell hole."

Myron followed the sound of his voice to a waist-high stone cylinder with a pool of shallow water in the center.

"Goes through twenty-odd swatches of burlap to filter large contaminates." Coyote Man pointed to just below the surface of the water. "Makes its way through a layer of sand, then a deep layer of coal dust to filter the hazardous garbage." He reached down and scooped a bowl of water where it trickled out at the base of the stones. "Got to boil it after that. I might eventually turn green from it, but I'm still here."

In Myron's estimation, the crazy man on the rim who

thought himself a coyote was far more intelligent than most people that Myron had encountered. He looked peculiar, spoke with a strange affectation, and lived without the company of others, yet he set Myron at ease. He could never forgive Coyote Man for stealing him away when Sindra needed him the most, but Myron did need water, and he needed a plan.

"This water's been cleaned and boiled." He grabbed the water skin from Myron and scooped from another shallow pool adjacent to the filters. "Come on."

Myron followed Coyote Man to the map on the wall.

"Right here." Coyote Man pointed to the map, to a spot in the fence on the other side of the compound, a place Myron had never set foot. "Followed a coyote to a hole in the fence." He nodded to the water skin. "It'll take you a day or two to get over there. Just so you don't try to sneak off without me, I'm going to head over to that contraption and wait for you there. You get yourself killed or captured, or don't return, well I'm taking my chances on figuring the thing out."

Coyote Man headed to the fire and scooped what was left of the stew for Myron. "Eat all you can." He picked out a sinewy piece from the pot and slung it into his mouth before handing Myron the scoop.

"One thing. Trip wires. Over there on the other side where the Gorge narrows a bit."

"The Gorge narrows?"

"Yeah, and they have the place extra guarded. That's where the hole in the fence is. You can tell the trip wires, they look like little twigs sticking up out of the ground. Set one of those off and you'll have company quick."

"Okay."

"Most important thing. Listen to me, boy." Coyote Man grabbed Myron's shoulders and lowered him to eye level. "This hole isn't obvious. If it was, patrols would have found it and fixed it. That fence goes below ground a ways, see. Can't really get under it. But this coyote went down into a crack in the earth about twenty feet from the razor wire, and I saw him come up on the other side half a minute later. Look for an old pump station. About a hect beyond that."

"How do you know it was the same coyote?"

"It's Nick. I call him that 'cause he has half an ear nicked off."

Myron thought about the goat foxes he'd seen, scrawny and wily. "How will I fit in a coyote hole?"

"This hole is pretty big. Don't think it was dug by any coyote."

Myron slung the water skin over his shoulder and crawled out of the cave. He walked in the direction of the old pump station, but not wanting to waste any more time, he began to jog.

CHAPTER 10

Sindra's eyes, now crusted shut and weather-bitten, pried open at the shriek of a rusty hinge. Through the slits of her vision, she made out two ghosts and a throng of slogs gathered around the shirker coop with anticipation, their murmurings sounding much like the clackety-clack of a train as it slowed into the depot.

A discipline rod prodded her in the shoulder. Sindra moaned, and the crowd gasped. "She's alive!" Shouts from the crowd made her eardrums throb.

Two ghosts peeled away the cover that had saved her from a frozen death, a personal blanket that she remembered came from Errol and two heavy saddle blankets that she had no memory of receiving. Between moments of consciousness and darkness, Sindra caught the blur of faces and puffs of gray clouds shrouding the smokestacks, heard whispers and scoffs, as the ghosts pulled her from the coop.

When she commanded her muscles to move, they

did not obey, sending only pain in response, so the ghosts plopped her onto a litter, one normally used for carrying expired people to the dead yard, and hauled her away. The world wobbled as they transported her through the astounded crowd of slogs, all of whom expressed signs of outrage or relief and nothing in between.

During her trip back to the Industry Administration building, passing under the gargoyles on sentry, the way the light played with the shadows around her, a fear germinated in her semiconscious brain that she might have expired during her trial and would soon find her way to the hellfires of the chasm, the Great Above having abandoned her. Sindra believed that Cardiff, the Custodian spirit of children, turned a blind eye at the age of knowledge, which Sindra had already passed, and Larande, the Custodian who guided the spirits of all women to the Great Above, perished in the last war, from exhaustion at the weight of too many souls to escort. Sindra had no one.

Once again before the administrator's clerk, Sindra rolled onto the floor from the litter that carried her. Unable to move, she lay on her back, relieved to have her legs fully extended, and stared at the blurry ceiling four stories above her, at the murals of healthy slogs working, smiling, in colors Sindra had never seen at Jonesbridge, with a sun that shot golden rays from the center all the way to the corners. She had observed images like these once in the train depot of a long forgotten town. There, too, the murals featured these bold, though faded colors, straight lines, symmetrical, with ornate machines, and drawings of hammers that could hew a mountainside. Looking at these paintings did spark some pride in that part of Sindra that was a worker.

A ghost behind her pulled apart Sindra's lips and poured several gulps of water into her mouth. Though it threatened to come up, she swallowed hard to keep it down, and her vision began to strengthen along with her confidence that she had not died in the shirker coop. The agony of sore muscles replaced the floating sensation of near death, and the air smelled once again of soot and ash.

The spectacle of her survival persisted in the form of a formal announcement from the Superintendent of Industry. When Sindra heard his voice, she hoped that, being in this building, he would make a personal appearance, that she would see if he really did look like all the posters that depicted him with a grand mustache and hair slicked back on his head, muscles bulging through his work shirt. Instead, after scanning in all directions, finally with enough energy to move her neck, she saw nothing, only heard the grainy voice she listened to every day on the factory floor during morning admonition.

"We have all submitted to incalculable sacrifice," the Superintendent began.

"Stand up," the ghost behind her insisted.

When she tried to lift her head, the ceiling spun into a whirl of color. The ghosts hoisted her to her feet. Her head fell onto her shoulder, her legs so limp the ghosts could not let go of her.

"Though you shirked your duty, your fellow workers have spared you. That means you still have production value and are exonerated of your shirking charges." The voice, as if emanating from nowhere, ceased, leaving only a dwindling echo in the cavernous space above her.

The administrator's clerk motioned Sindra to step

forward. "That takes care of the shirking and ration theft. As far as the interrogation for the murder, the Superintendent needs no further information. The murderer has been identified. Report to reorientation and then return to your duties."

Identified? Sindra heard the words, but in her current state found them hard to process. Relief or despair, the implications braided together as though they formed a rope around her neck. She'd spent four days in the coop. A lot had happened in that time. The clerk instructed the ghosts to give Sindra an extra swig of water and a protein stick before they led her off to the stretcher for reorientation, to go from being folded up in a cage for four days to being pulled to her limits.

Not until dusk did Sindra make it back to 14-C, to her domicile and cot that felt to her like a bed of clouds. The warm sun on a sandy strip of coastline lulled her to sleep with the white birds that Myron had described cawing over the sounds of crashing water.

The next morning, after nearly twelve hours of sleep, Sindra filed through the factory door ahead of the 7:00 A.M. siren wail. She endured entrance procedures as she did every day, only more sore and nauseous, still missing Myron's face across the factory floor, a sight that used to comfort her as the hours on the line seemed like they would drag to a halt. The more her pregnancy progressed, the more it felt as though everyone in the entire factory had their eyes fixed on her instead of the south wall banner. She could feel the collective stare of her shift mates—Rolf and even the ghosts that guarded the door.

Women, Old Nickel once explained, had always relied

on each other for help and counsel during the childbearing process. She had said that women were of one soul when it came to the tribulations of bringing new life into the world. If you didn't have a mother or an aunt or a grandmother, any woman who had birthed a child was family in that time. But the women in Jonesbridge couldn't give her counsel. They hadn't experienced it themselves. Sindra now had no one to ask about how she was supposed to feel—if it was normal that she felt sick all the time, felt scared and happy and exhausted before the day had even begun. There was no one there to tell her that everything was fine, that she would make it through, only the hope that bad things pass in time.

Standing at attention, eyes on the Industry banner, the Superintendent of Industry ushered in the minute of silence for fallen countrymen and then began his admonition for the shift.

"The news today gives me great pause," the Superintendent said, and cleared his throat. "How many lives have we lost? How much have we all sacrificed in the name of our country, the very symbol for what we hold dear. Our values, our collective spirits. Today, I must report that, while your countrymen are dying on the battlefield, while your countrymen toil in the mines and on factory floors and endure the elements and hardships of war, one among you has put himself over all of us, you, me, the dead and dying." He paused as he often did when the news was supposed to be shocking.

On this particular morning, the Superintendent's words alarmed Sindra. She wanted to cover her ears and ignore the rest of his statement and fight the reality of what she feared he was about to say.

"We have identified the murderer of the dutiful civil guard," the Superintendent continued as a squad of Civil Guards marched into the salvage factory. Six of them ushered down the center of the factory floor in two columns of three, heading straight for Sindra's workstation. She couldn't believe they'd released her only yesterday, told she was no longer a suspect, and here they were again, about to reignite her dread. She looked around the room. All eyes followed the ghosts, leading right to her.

Rolf stood beside her, as if to aid in her apprehension. Two ghosts joined him from behind and two stood at his side, ignoring Sindra, and instead snapped Rolf's legs and hands into shackles.

"What are you doing? It's not *me*." Rolf squirmed in the shackles. "I didn't kill him! It's not me."

The mouth of every slog on the factory floor gaped at the sight of their floor boss in chains, but Rolf maintained his innocence, repeating "I didn't do it," as they led him away. The oaf who'd berated her and yelled in her face, a man who Sindra had thought never cared whether she lived or died, had stepped in behind her and cleaned up her and Myron's mess? She found it hard to believe. It wasn't possible.

Unlike the Superintendent, who they never saw in person, the salvage factory administrator, Cyril, made his presence known often. He stepped down a set of stairs in the corner of the room. With his hands locked behind his back, he scrutinized every slog on the line, stopping periodically, often returning to a slog he'd seen earlier. He halted his visual interrogation in front of Saul whose puffed-out chest hinted at his anticipation of what the administrator would say.

"Saul." He held out Rolf's processing clipboard. "*You*

are the new salvage day shift foreman." Sindra noticed an exchange between the two, a silent acknowledgement as Saul's eyes locked with the administrator's, as if the promotion were preordained. He turned to address the entire factory. "This is your new foreman." He held his hand over Saul's head. "Cross him—cross me." Sindra looked away when Saul glanced at her with a crooked grin he couldn't conceal. She could think of few people worse than Saul for the job, dreading the first time he berated her work behind a smarmy glare. Saul couldn't even cut a fused bushing off of an overloader shaft. Sindra hated Rolf, but not so much as a person, just as a foreman, the way she hated every foreman. They were bossy and loud and abusive, but the good ones looked out for their crews. Saul had all of the bad traits of a foreman and none of the good ones. He was like the moistened chaff used in ration bread. Rolf, at least, had a mechanical aptitude worthy of respect.

From the grainy speaker, the Superintendent resumed his admonition. "We also have the matter of a duty shirker. We have combed the canal and searched the grounds for his remains to no avail. So it is now a matter of ordinance that anyone who knows the whereabouts of Myron Daw will be equally repudiated in the eyes of the law if such information is not disclosed."

Sindra's stomach whirled, first at the mention of Myron's name, imagining that he had actually made it, what he must have looked like, sailing across the Gorge in his airship filled with hot air from a pan of smoldering coal he had salted away for months. She could see his chiseled face, shrouded by smoke and ash and snow, gazing into the mountains ahead with a vision of the ocean driving him, his propeller spinning through the clouds.

She wondered if he thought about her, if he pined for her, but she imagined he hadn't been able to expand his machine to fit them both. If he hadn't gone on alone, if he had loved her as he promised he did, they would have tumbled out of the sky together, the airship unable to hold the extra weight and they would have perished, together, at the bottom of the Gorge. She assured herself of this. But he hadn't even said goodbye.

Sindra remembered little from her shift other than her anger at being left behind yet again, first by her family as a child, and now by Myron, and that her anger had somehow melted into pity and despair, emotions as worthless as a toothless rock lizard. On the march back to 14-C, she felt as though she were floating above herself, looking down at a double-file line of pitiful slogs all waiting for someone else to feed them.

Back at 14-C, Saul had a smug look on his face. "Looks like Myron turned out to be a loose wheel," he proclaimed as he passed Sindra in the swill pen. Sindra decided not to respond. "You're fortunate," he added, not taking his eyes from her abdomen. "But fortune's no substitute for duty."

Sindra took her ration to the corner of the swill pen and sat in the dirt. After a moment, Errol joined her. She observed his peculiar mannerisms, the way he hopped on his crutch, only a partial man, all the while acting as though he had the strength of ten men. She didn't know if she could trust this one-legged stranger who had arrived suddenly from out *there* as if he'd fallen from the sky, but he had saved her life in the coop. She had no choice.

"There's something off about you," Errol said. "I'd say I

know what it is. You have a problem, don't you?" He nodded at Sindra's stomach. "I think Saul's onto it, too."

"What are you talking about?"

"You've been in that cage for four days. You're looking more like the rest of us now, but you've still got more meat on you than what you should. Healthy enough to catch the eye of any real man left in this place." He continued to study her. "Relations of a carnal nature have been suspended for the common good. That's what they told me. Keep your mind on your work, Mule-man."

Sindra nodded.

"The doc will find out soon enough when you get bigger." He leaned closer and pulled his finger across his throat.

Sindra had been so excited to escape with Myron that she hadn't thought about anything beyond the day. She wanted to keep her womanhood at any cost.

"I know how—*where* you can have that problem taken care of."

"What do you mean, taken care of?"

"You know," his head swayed as he tried to coax the answer out of her. "End it."

The thought of ending her pregnancy made her want to cry. Everything she'd hoped for had dissipated in recent days, and as much as she had dreamed of having a baby, it wouldn't be possible to do without Myron's help getting her over the Gorge and out of Jonsebridge. Errol was right. If she waited any longer, if they discovered she was pregnant, Doc would perform the sterilization procedure again, and this time it would work. If she ended it now, kept her secret that she wasn't barren, she could someday have a child.

"How?"

"Well, here's the thing. I saved your keister in the coop. Damn near choked on my own spit giving you my water. And I'm gonna help you keep your womanhood. But I know the only person that could have done that to you was a ghost," he nodded to her abdomen. "So, now I need *your* help. Some extra rations from time to time."

Her help? Not only could he have her extra rations, she would gladly trade places with that one-legged mule-tender. She could give him one of her good legs and he could spend his nights half awake wondering when they would come to satisfy their desires on him. "Just extra rations?"

"And if you get the nerve to make another run for it, you have to take me along."

Sindra considered their trek through the tunnel, the crawling and jumping, knee-deep mud, swimming through muck, and whatever else they would have faced if they'd gone farther out there. "I don't think you could make it."

"Oh, I'm a gimp, and I'm getting on in years, but I can hop and roll faster than you think I can."

"There's nothing out there. No food. No clean water. Only a noxious pit that goes all the way around this place. Myron had a plan. I don't. "

"You don't have much time. We'll take care of your problem tonight, after bed check."

Only a day and a half removed from the shirker coop, the idea that she would sneak out of her domicile again so soon and risk something even worse made her ill, but someday having a child was a dream she would not jeopardize.

The excruciating wait for bed check revived the excitement she'd felt the first time she sneaked out to the chapel with Myron. He'd built up her hopes and torn them down. Losing him felt like she'd lost herself, making her wish they'd never met at all, until his dreams and his face wormed their way back into her mind. Waiting and pacing for another risky foray, this time with Errol, pushed her to pretend she was meeting Myron instead to make the whole process more fun, the way Myron made everything.

After bed check, Sindra navigated the spotlights the way she had the night she and Myron escaped, knowing that if they came to ravage her tonight and she wasn't in her domicile, she would lose everything. She dodged the ghosts on patrol and spotted Errol, who gave her a nod and stepped into the shadow of the archway to the main road. Errol led Sindra to the road that connected the extinct village of Old Town Jonesbridge to the domicile quads.

Sindra saw the buildings of Old Town, down in the valley, from the path to her factory every morning. It had always intrigued her, and though Old Jonesbridge was locked up inside the compound with the factories and domiciles, it was off limits to slogs.

"I'm the mule man. Between shifts, I care for the mules, among other things." He pointed to a crumbling clock tower that once tolled over the bustling village of Jonesbridge. "Well, that's where they keep the mules. I can be seen walking this road. You can't, so keep quiet."

Sindra followed instructions, walking quietly behind Errol, who hopped on his crutch. Even though the path was dark, it was out in the open, and it made Sindra nervous. She dropped to her knees to keep out of sight at the slightest hint of a ghost on patrol or a search light until they rounded a bend where the path widened into a road. Pangs of rail-walker nostalgia struck her when they finally reached the cluster of buildings that resembled a town.

Old Town Jonesbridge consisted of a network of narrow bricked streets pocked with craters, flanked by defunct shops that clung to their ancient charm. Some signs still hung above gutted structures, as though no one had told them they were no longer needed, pictures of a coffee cup or a pair of boots and man in a western hat holding a mug. Footprints of extinct streetlights, robbed for their metal, led to the center of town where the clock tower oversaw it all, crowned with a giant Pegasus weathervane, though nothing of its mechanisms remained. These were all familiar sights to Sindra who'd explored many bygone towns along the rails. It even possessed a different smell than the rest of the Jonesbridge complex, an earthy scent like damp wood, something she associated with the way a spider web might smell.

"Okay, let's go." He positioned his crutch and squeezed through an opening in the wall into a dark shell of a structure. "Follow me. Hold the back of my smock."

"Where are we going?"

He glanced back at her, a flicker of a smirk at the corner of his mouth.

"To see Lalana, of course."

CHAPTER 11

Though he'd only been gone four days, as he returned to the compound for Sindra, Myron no longer recognized 14-C as his home. After he'd tasted freedom out on the rim, everything about Jonesbridge had changed in his mind. He tiptoed up the stairs, keeping out of sight. Passing by rooms, he expected to hear morning noises, groans of awakening day shifters hauling off the cot, clicks and clanks of stove doors opening and closing, but he realized he had made it too late, after the day shift had already begun. Instead, he saw a line of slogs shuffling back from night shift.

Myron ran to his domicile where he noticed a strip of tape across the door that stretched from one wall to the other. He stopped short of ripping the tape, realizing they had set a trap for him, so he headed for Sindra's room to wait for her until the day shift ended. The return trek into the compound had taken all the fight he had left for the moment, dodging patrols on the rim, trip wires, crawling though a dark fissure under the fence where coyotes had setup housekeeping. He'd sustained a bite on the nose and a deep wound on his hand where teeth marks remained, but stalking the nighttime like an animal had suited Myron. He'd experienced the simple freedom an animal enjoys every day, coming and going as the elements dictated, and though he had never given much credence to the spirit Custodians, he thought there might actually be a coyote Custodian spirit that nobody spoke of, one that he'd now bonded with in blood.

On the sixth and final floor of 14-C, he found her door and turned the handle, opening it to an empty room. He checked the corridor again and entered her quarters. Under the cot, he saw her possessions. She had plenty of coal and an extra smock laid out by the basin, ready for her next shift. Myron sat on the cot and smelled her blanket, a scent he had kept with him since the last time they were together.

All his dreams now possessed her face. If he took her from his dreams, they disappeared, no more dreams, no more beach or palms trees or creatures of the sea, no more escape plan, no need to do anything at all. The nagging fear that Sindra may have taken the blame for the ghost's murder led Myron to one conclusion after another, all leading to horrible visions of her freshly limed body lying in the deadyard. He had not seen a murder in his time in Jonesbridge and had no idea as to the punishment. If only he'd looked up sooner during their ration raid or managed to fight off Coyote Man before he struck, Sindra would still be with him. They might even have made it across the Gorge by now.

Every hour he added to the wait amplified his nightmares as he wondered what he would do, how he could go on if Sindra did not open the door and walk into this room after her shift. The day he smuggled out her star, the longest day in Jonesbridge, now took second place to today as he sat on Sindra's cot, holding her smock, willing her to somehow appear, a day that finally came to an end when the official curfew siren sounded. He waited. When he could wait no longer, Myron cracked open the door and noticed a shadow on the corridor wall, praying for Sindra's face to appear. Instead, he looked up to see Saul.

Their eyes met briefly, first as shift mates and fellow countrymen, both out past curfew, empathetic, then as predator and prey. "Shirker!" Saul yelled, pointing at Myron. "Myron Daw!"

Myron shoved Saul aside on his way through the door, effortlessly, the way an overloader bladed passed a stack of garbage in the salvage pit. He ran to the walkway, stopping at the rail, staring down into the swill pen.

"Myron Daw!" Saul screamed again. Myron saw as many as six ghosts scrambling for the stairs. He ran to the end of the row of quarters and glanced over the rail, ghosts everywhere—all running for him.

"Myron Daw," Saul cried again, standing at attention, his outstretched finger pointing at Myron. Ghosts ran from both ends of the corridor, planning to sandwich Myron on the top floor of the domicile quad. The only way out was down.

Six floors up, Myron threw one leg over the rail and hurled himself over. The air whooshed by his ears. He lost his breath as he landed in the grasp of the suicide nets that surrounded the domiciles on the second floor. He struggled to make it to the edge, hoping to escape into the darkness, but his feet got tangled in the net. He tugged harder. Ghosts ran down the stairs on either side of him.

Myron freed his legs and rolled off the net, falling from the second floor, landing hard on his side. He crawled toward the dark space between the quads, finally getting up to run when they closed in on him, discipline rods drawn. He steadied himself and tightened his stomach in preparation for the blows from the rod, which came sooner than he expected. One, two in the stomach, three on the back. Then he folded to the ground. He squirmed, clutching his ribs at the feet of several ghosts until they lifted him to his feet and led him to the administration complex at the heart of Jonesbridge.

· · ·

Myron waited in a dark room with a slit of light emerging from under the door. No one questioned him or accused him of anything. He just sat there imagining one horrible thing after another that must have happened to Sindra in the four days he was gone, going through all of the things he could have done differently, itemizing his failures, and realizing that yet again, he'd made the wrong decision. Sitting and waiting, anticipating, his fear grew until the door opened and four ghosts hoisted him to his feet and led him out.

At the end of a corridor, Myron passed through a shadowy doorway, his hands bound with binding twine. Ahead of him lay a narrow passageway, wide enough for his shoulders but too low for him to proceed without ducking his head. The march came to an end in a cavernous chamber bisected by a canal that ran underneath the walls on either side. A mill wheel three times Myron's height sat partway submerged in the center of the waterway. Chains dangled from the wheel that glistened in the torchlight.

The sight of Rolf, shackled, standing by the wheel shocked Myron as he rounded the corner, crossing the canal on a catwalk flanked by two guards. Myron stood at attention, watching as they escorted Rolf up a ladder to the top of the wheel where they secured him longwise along the curve with chains. "I didn't kill anybody," Rolf insisted, jerking at the chains as the ghosts tightened them.

The ghost in a control room pulled a lever. The wheel spun, taking Rolf head first into the murky water where he stopped, completely submerged. Myron shook his head and backed away as the ghosts forced him onto the top of the wheel, where he fought until his knees buckled, held fast with the pull of the chains. Water dripped from the chains, reminding Myron that these restraints, the ones clenching down on his thighs and chest just came from under water, where they would certainly return. Still in the open air, still taking breaths, Myron tried to prepare himself for the horror Rolf was experiencing at that same moment, when the water would rob him of breath.

Myron had learned to swim in the stream behind his grandfather's house, in waters yellow with sulfur and mud, but he'd never learned to hold his breath and put his head under. That silent breath, hearing his own heartbeat in his chest with a suffocating wet blanket all around him frightened him, so much that he never went into water too deep to stand in. He'd experienced the horror when he went under helping Sindra across the canal, the chemicals in his nose, the burn in his lungs. As the wheel began to turn, his head aiming downward toward the water, Myron sucked in a deep breath and squeezed his eyes shut.

The wheel creaked. As Rolf emerged from the water on the other side he gasped just as the water swallowed Myron. A white coldness enveloped him, as though he had stepped into a frozen sun. He heard voices, Rolf's shouts above him, but he couldn't make out the words. He held his breath until his chest might split apart and the wheel began to turn. When he came up on the other side he opened his mouth as wide as he could and bit at air, like a fish on land.

"Myron Daw, you stand accused of the crimes of shirking four days, possession of books and other contraband, and the murder of Civil Colleague 5432."

"But he was alive when I saw him," Myron yelled still catching his breath. "I was protecting Sindra. I didn't kill him."

The wheel rotated. Myron's head started toward the water, chains still dripping from his last trip. As the rush of water bubbled around his ears, he heard Rolf's voice. He tried to parse the muted syllables, wondering what Rolf was saying, if he was telling them Myron had done it, if Rolf was a suspect or a witness. Without air to his brain, Myron couldn't think. He could only concentrate on not breathing in the water until the wheel turned again.

"This process will stop when one of you confesses."

"I hit the guard. But he was still alive. He started to chase me. I didn't kill him."

The wheel turned. Myron's head ached as the water rushed around him, his hair suspended in the liquid.

"Why were you behind the domicile quad?"

"They were ravaging Sindra. I had to help her."

"Where did you go after you hit the guard?"

"Back to my domicile."

"Rolf says you chased the guard."

"How would he know? Rolf wasn't there."

The wheel began to turn, and Myron realized he had made a fatal error in his panic. "Wait, wait," he yelled, sucking in a breath right before he went under. Above him Rolf's voice, deep and urgent sank down through the water in dull bursts. Concentrating on keeping his breath, Myron tried to replace the darkness with Sindra's face. When the wheel turned again it stopped midway, with both he and Rolf out of the water on the sides of the wheel, Rolf upside down on his way into the water, Myron head up. He could hardly hear over his own gasping.

"Rolf Bucker, Myron Daw has implicated you in the murder."

"What? No. I didn't, Rolf. I swear."

"Myron Daw, Rolf has implicated you."

"No, I didn't. Myron, tell them what you told me. About a wild man," Rolf yelled, upside down on the other side. His voice crackled, a sound Myron had never heard come out of Rolf's mouth. "Please tell them, Myron!"

After a few moments of silence, a door swung open to the control room. Two men remained at the controls, an administrator of some sort and a ghost, but the man who walked through the door Myron recognized as Cyril, the salvage factory administrator.

"A wild man?" The administrator asked as he glanced over to the control room, his voice almost a whisper. "What sort of wild man?"

"Ask Myron. He knows."

"I don't know," Myron snapped. "A Coyote Man."

The administrator stepped up beside Myron and pulled on the chain, nodding to the water. "What wild man?"

"He lives on the rim. I don't know where."

The salvage administrator raised his hand, and the wheel began to turn. Myron rose around. A splash signaled Rolf's entry back into the water. Two ghosts unchained Myron from the top of the wheel. He climbed down the ladder where the salvage administrator waited. He shook his hands, trying to get feeling back into his fingers, now off the wheel and out of the cold water, finally unbound.

"Where did you see this wild man?"

Myron couldn't take his eyes off the part of the wheel that was still under water, expecting it to rotate up so that they could unchain Rolf, but the wheel did not move.

"What did he look like?" The salvage administrator slammed Myron against the wall. "Tell me."

"I don't know. He's covered in hair. And he wears goat fox skins. He's been out there a while." Myron held his hand out at nose level. "About this tall I guess."

The wheel still hadn't moved. Bubbles surfaced around the edge. "What about Rolf?"

"What's this about?" the other administrator joined them. "All this talk about a wild man. We have our murderer." He pointed to the bottom of the wheel. "Let's go."

With his eyes fixed of Rolf's silhouette in the murky water, Myron noticed the chains stop moving from struggle, the froth around the wheel had ceased, and the water grew still. Rolf had paid someone else's price.

"Let's go see about this wild man. If it's true, we may have more problems. Get a squad, and Myron will take us out to find him." The other administrator slapped Myron's legs and arms into adjoined shackles and led him to the two ghosts by the door.

Emerging from the wheelhouse chamber, the brightness outdoors stung Myron's eyes. He looked up and saw the sun perched high in a blue sky. He squinted and looked away, turning around to the soot-stained fortress of red brick behind him. Steel refinery #4 had gone silent. No boilers humming, no motors turning, and above its towering smokestacks—no smoke. Same with #3 and #2 beside it. No lights, no electrical hum. Nothing, just hundreds of workers filing out of the buildings in bewilderment.

"Come on. Get going." The ghost to Myron's left gave him a shove.

The strap that joined his ankle shackles had just enough slack for Myron to scuffle in half strides as he led the team of four ghosts and the salvage administrator out to Coyote Man, though Myron had planned to lead them anywhere but where he thought Coyote Man would be. With each step he heard in his mind the whimpering howl of coyotes yapping at each other late at night. Unlike other dog-types, like the wolves of the legends, coyotes didn't possess great strength or even speed. They were opportunists. They made do, adapted to a changing environment, utilized what others had discarded—much like salvage. In this ability, they were free and strong. Now that he had awakened his inner coyote, he could feel the bristles standing up on the back of his neck. In his time in Jonesbridge he had never seen the sky this clear and the factories this silent, a sun so bright that it warmed the skin on his arms. Something was not right.

They left the compound through the supply depot gate, the same spot he had last seen Sindra, and when they reached the area near the cave entrance, Myron collapsed onto a boulder and pointed with his bound hands. "I don't know. It all looks the same out here." He took a deep breath. His chest still ached. "Maybe it's that way." He pointed in the opposite direction of Coyote Man's cave.

After an hour of Myron leading the squad in circles the head ghost stopped them. "This is a waste of time. Keep watch on this hill. Eyes peeled for for a wild man to show his face. You first," the head ghost said pointing to another ghost with a black stripe on his shoulder. "Three of you rotate in eight hour shifts until I give the word."

The ghost assigned to the first shift, a man not much older than Myron, had a worried expression. "Just one of us?" He cleared his throat. "Against a *wild man*?"

The head ghost sighed and ripped a pistol from a hidden holster under his smock. Only the Defense Administration had guns, or so Myron thought. The head ghost spun the chamber and locked it into place with a click. He pulled the discipline rod from the other ghost's hand and handed him the pistol. "There's one in the chamber—a *real* bullet. If he shows up. Shoot him right in the eye."

The ghost turned the gun over in his hand, inspecting it with wide eyes. "H-how do I do that exactly?"

"Just point this end," he said, nudging the end of the barrel, "where you want to shoot and squeeze the curved part by the grip."

"Okay." The ghost sat down on a boulder.

"And stay out of sight." The head ghost sighed, shaking his head. "If there really is a wild man out here, he'll be cautious."

"Wait," the salvage administrator said, confronting the

the head ghost. "We want to question him. Do *not* kill the wild man. Do not kill him."

"Okay, disable him for capture and questioning. But if you can't detain him, kill him." The head ghost shot the administrator a suspicious glance.

It worried Myron how close the ghost on watch really was to the cave entrance, but he had managed to keep them looking in the wrong direction.

Chaos greeted Myron when the other three ghosts and the administrator returned him to Jonesbridge through the supply depot. Under a clear sky, bright sunlight reflected off the railroad tracks. Dozens of slogs in disarray scuttled out in the open, unproductive. Myron recognized one of the people right away, Millie, his commissary clerk at 14-C. She looked frantic, and Millie never seemed the type to lose her cool.

"What's going on?" The head ghost barked at Mille. She paced outside the ration distribution bakery behind an empty ration pushcart, her journal tucked under her arm. At least twenty other commissary clerks stood in a similar fashion, fidgeting and hopping from one foot to another to keep warm, all with empty ration carts.

"It's *closed*," Millie barked back, pointing to the ration bakery, a warehouse adjacent to the supply depot that smelled either of baking bread or entrails, depending on the time of day.

"Locked up tight." The clerk for 11-D, gave his cart a nudge.

Myron thought that if they had ever gnawed the flesh off a coyote bone, felt the surge of nature running through their blood, they'd forget all about that pureed mash, hit the wild, and never look back.

"All right, let's break it up here." Two more ghosts walked up with discipline rods drawn. Four others followed closely behind. "Bakery's closed today. Come back tomorrow."

"What'll we give out for rations?" Millie asked.

"Slogs work until someone tells them to stop," the ghost on Myron's right said. "Food or not. Anyone who has a problem, give them this." The ghost pounded Millie's ration cart with a blow so hard that it broke the shelves into pieces.

A civil guard with four black stripes on his shoulder, a captain, came out to the center of a growing throng of idle workers. He held up a megaphone to speak. "The Superintendent of Industry has an announcement."

"Is the war over?" A voice shouted from the crowd.

"The war's over?"

"Oh, mercy, heavenly day."

"No," the captain shouted. "The war is *not* over."

From the top of the stanchion in the supply depot, the speaker crackled with static ahead of a rare public message.

"Fellow countrymen, fellow workers, shift mates and friends," the Superintendent of Industry began. "Three days ago," his voiced echoed through the maze of redbrick walls, "I received a dispatch that our main source of coal fell under enemy attack. Our forces have mobilized and we have every confidence that we will secure the region. We have not taken delivery of coal for two days. Our reserves have been diverted to Munitions, but that will last only two more days. The Civil Guard has the authority to dispose of anyone not cooperating with emergency procedures."

Gasps erupted from the crowd.

"Effective immediately, in teams supervised by your shift

foreman and accompanying Civil Guards, you are charged to scour the countryside bound by the Jonesbridge Gorge and return anything that our fireboxes can burn as fuel. This means every shin pine, every weed, stick or log, dry grass, and scrap of wood from Old Town. I want to see this valley look as though you've given it a morning shave. With our numbers we will fill our fireboxes! With our numbers, we will continue production!" His voice grew louder until the speaker box cut out in the middle of his words. "With ou... n...bers, we will k...p ...ur troops supplied and take back our ...oal!"

Myron's entire body weakened as he imagined every worker in Jonesbridge scouring the countryside, ripping it to shreds top to bottom, destroying the old chapel, finding Coyote Man's cave and unearthing the bunker with Myron's flying machine inside.

"What should we do with *him*?" The ghost tapped Myron with his jerry-rod.

"He's no murderer, but throw him in the coop for shirking. Then get with a group and get firebox fuel like the Super said."

CHAPTER 12

Blanketed by darkness, Errol stopped and knelt down. Holding Sindra's hand, he patted the ground, grappling with something on the floor. The boards creaked around them when he pulled open a door in the floor. "Careful. These steps are narrow and steep."

Sindra climbed down the steps sideways to fit in the narrow passage, following the contours of the wall as the staircase curved. Ahead of her, the sound of Errol's crutch landed, followed by the plop of his foot behind it, until even that fell silent. Dim light emerged as she rounded the last corner of the staircase. At the bottom of the stairs, Errol's face flickered above a candle.

"Where are we?" An odor of waste and illness met her at the bottom of the stairs.

"Cellar. People in the old days used to keep fermentations down here. Quickest way to the stables without being seen." He nodded to shadowy recesses in the stone corridor. "It's also the quarantine."

A series of alcoves that once housed wine flickered with candlelight, accompanied by sounds of coughing and hacking. "This is where you go if you get really sick—wet lung, trench mouth. On half rations, since they're not working." Errol pulled his smock over his nose. "Cover your face."

Sindra followed his lead. The woman to her right coughed, sounding as though her insides might gurgle out of her mouth.

"Sometimes they recover and return to work. Most times they don't."

Errol pulled some bread and a couple of protein sticks from his smock. He broke the bread and handed it to a woman with swollen eyes. She looked up at him, the whites of her eyes the color of blood.

"Why here?" Sindra whispered.

"In case they're contagious."

Sindra panicked.

"This is part of my duties as mule caretaker. Bring the sick folks their half ration." He shrugged. "Close to the stables, I guess. Anyway, how do you think I was able to keep you alive? I brought you some of what these folks were supposed to get."

He continued to dole out rations. "Way I see it, if you get some extra rations, you owe these slogs." He filled a cup of water next to the woman, careful to keep the canteen from opening and touching it. "I'm a pious man of sorts. I didn't like short-shrifting them. But you're alive and that's what matters now."

They surfaced through a doorway in a freestanding

wall, balanced by the sheer will of its bricks without any building behind it to hold it. Sindra could smell the stables before she could see them as she followed Errol along a path through several more alleyways until they reached the long line of wooden lean-tos and a corral where twenty or more mules milled around, some with their heads in a trough. In a separate corral, three horses snorted at the gate. The donkey stood like a statue in a smaller pen.

"Lala. You got a visitor," Errol said, his voice a coarse whisper.

Behind them, a stable door swung open. The stall had been swept clean of its hay and had a chair and table in the corner near a cot. A dark woman draped in rags, older than anyone in Jonesbridge, ambled through the door opening. She walked as though she had a limp in both legs, grunting slightly with each step. "What are you poking around out here this time of night for?"

"She needs your expertise," he said pointing to Sindra. "With a medical condition."

"Looks healthy to me." Lalana flattened her hand against Sindra's forehead.

Errol reached over and lifted Sindra's smock all the way to her breast. "Look."

"Oh my." Lalana turned around and ambled into the stable. "Well, come on inside."

She lit two candles and plopped down in her chair. In the flickering yellow light Sindra could see Lalana's face. She had skin the color of a rusted poke-iron and round cheeks with mesmerizing narrow eyes in the shape of eggs. From a cabinet behind her, Lalana reached for a purple root, pushing aside jars and boxes of assorted shapes and sizes.

She grabbed a triangular bottle filled with greenish liquid and poured some into a bowl, measuring out extra after she eyed Sindra from top to bottom. "I'm going to whip you up a black whisper." She broke off a hunk of the purple root and began to grind it into a stringy soup in the bowl. "This'll stop that life growing inside you."

"A black whisper?" Sindra asked. She was relieved that this visit to Lalana would not involve surgery, that all she had to do was drink something and it would all be done with. "What is it?" Worn boxes lined her shelves, each labeled with letters Sindra could not read.

Lalana positioned the bowl over the candle until the mixture bubbled. "Oh, a little of this, a little of that. A smatter of Viper thistle. Spit of Hornwood extract." She reached for a red box on the shelf full of leafy vines and crumbled some into the bowl. "Bit of billet thistle for any pain." Then Lalana stuffed her own cheeks with a wad of billet thistle and took a deep breath. "Might taste a little ripe at first. Probably won't sleep too well tonight. Then no more *problem*."

Sindra watched Lalana mix the concoction, tossing in one thing after another, still doubtful about her decision.

"Okay. It's ready." Lalana handed Sindra the bowl. "Drink all of it. Quickly."

Sindra kissed her fingers and placed them on her abdomen, wishing the tiny him, or her, a safe trip to the Great Above. When Sindra took the bowl, the smell caused her to turn away. She pinched her nose, closed her eyes and gulped it down in three swallows, not allowing herself an opportunity to change her mind.

"That's it," Lalana whispered, reaching for the

empty bowl.

Sindra's lips puckered. The mixture tasted the way the stables smelled. She gasped for breath. "What now?"

"Wait."

"This is just awful," Sindra said. "So few people left in the world. We need more people. Just doesn't make sense."

Lalana pointed to Sindra. "That is the reason," she said clicking her tongue. "So we don't extinct ourselves like we did the animals. A slog baby, if it doesn't die right away, comes out deaf, blind, or missing limbs and such. Or it carries along invisible abnormalities." She bent down for a handful of dirt. "The earth is sick. It's changed us. You're a slog. Here for production and that's it."

Sindra's stomach ached, unsure of why she was sick, the black whisper or what Lalana had just told her. "You are a doctor, right?"

"When I was a girl, my daddy worked as an animal caretaker for a traveling menagerie. Shame. No animals left these days except beasts of burden, and there are precious few of those."

"Goat foxes," Errol corrected.

"Yeah, and some lizards and mice and such," Lalana added. "I'm speaking of the grand beasts." She held the bowl over the candle flame with a pair of tongs, sloshing it as the syrupy liquid bubbled and popped, boiling away the remaining fluid. "Those three horses over there." She point to the corral. "That's all I know that exist. Something happens to them, I don't know where to find more."

"I don't understand."

"Clean farmland. That's what we've been fighting over for decades. Some places weren't exposed to the things that alter your insides. Everyone else gets whatever food they can make out of this God-forgotten soil, because the damage has already been done."

"How do you know?"

"I'm an old woman." Her eyelids folded into wrinkles when she chuckled. "Before I came to Jonesbridge, I worked for the farms near Simonville, before the E'sters torched it. This *change* I'm telling you about isn't something you can clean." She clasped her hands together and sat them on the table. "Lordy, I don't know what our ancestors did to this earth. Bit by bit, like the birds and the grand beasts, people will fade away, too. Had to put a mule down the other day because it was born without most of its brain."

"So, even if I keep my secret, that I'm not sterile, I still won't be able to have a baby?"

Lalana's eyes jerked from staring into the corral to Sindra's eyes. "That baby," she said with a point to Sindra's abdomen, "had to be a product of relations with a ghost. They aren't as messed up on the inside as a slog. That child might have half a chance."

Sindra had buried the pain of the rapes, nurturing dreams of a future where she and Myron would escape and raise the baby together, as though their union had brought life into the world. When he left, she held hope that a baby could still be in her future somehow if no one found out she'd kept her womanhood, but if what Lalana told her was true, this might be her one and only chance at it, a fifty-fifty shot.

Sindra stumbled to the edge of the stable and stuck her fingers down her throat, tickling the back of her tongue until she heaved. The black whisper roiled in her stomach, rumbling up her throat.

"What are you doing?"

Errol ran over to Sindra to check on her. "I risked my neck to bring you out here."

"I know, I know," Sindra said as she continued to heave the purplish concoction onto the hay. She kept going, not satisfied she'd purged herself completely of the black whisper, not until dry heaves burned her throat. It had only sat in her stomach for a few moments. If she'd managed to vomit it up before it soured her baby, she held hope that she would mother her child in a matter of months. A fifty-fifty chance was one she wanted to take.

Sindra rested on the hay for a while before she willed herself to sit up. She'd been too young when her mother died to really get any sense of mothering and the sorts of things a mother does. The rail-walkers had taken on that role for Sindra, but they had a patina around their souls, like the old bronze that sometimes wound up on the salvage floor, as likely to wallop her as let any tenderness show through. They did drop bits and pieces of advice here and there, but mostly they looked out for themselves, they had to, surviving rails.

Sindra knew what advice Old Nickel would give her now—fight and die, or run away—her words to live by. The first half, *fight and die*, she'd told Sindra meant that if you stay and fight, either win the fight or die trying. The second half of that mantra, the *run away* part, Bug had told her that if she decided to run away she should always *scatter to survive*— harder to catch many solitary runners than a group in one spot. At least someone would get away. This time, she would not let anyone cage her up.

"Errol," Sindra said, "time for me to make good on our

bargain. I'll get you out of this compound. After that you're on your own."

His eyes narrowed and he turned to look at Lalana.

"Errol, what's this girl talking about?"

Sindra gave Errol a nod. "I owe him. I guess you can make it, even with only one leg, since you're some sort of war hero." Errol's presence had actually been a source of inspiration for everyone in 14-C. His tales of the world outside their factory compound, even horrific stories of war, reminded them all that there was still something going on somewhere else.

Lalana laughed, making the loose skin around her throat shake. "War hero? Is that what he told you?" She poked at him with the oat scoop. "This fool's afraid of a damn mule flea."

Errol lowered his head. "I lost my leg to a plow, not in the swamp. I invented some things." Errol grabbed his crutch. "But I *can* make it."

"A gimp and a liar. Great skills for getting across that rugged country."

Sindra considered the risks he took to bring her water and blankets in the coop and the sacrifice the quarantined slogs had endured and acknowledged that she did owe him. "Fine, but I'm not getting caught again."

"There's no leaving this compound," Lalana said.

"Sindra knows how."

"And if I can't get over the Gorge, I'll take my chances on the rim."

Lalana shook her head. "You really know a way out of this compound?"

She filled her medical bag. "I understand your desire. I

never had a child of my own, either. " She said pointing at the corral. "Except for helping a good many mules come into the world. But this is a big chance you're taking for fifty-fifty. You threw up that black whisper. Good chance you got that life still kicking inside you." She ambled up beside Errol carrying her medical bag. "What? You're not thinking of leaving *me* behind are you?" She asked Errol who looked away.

Sindra watched Errol limp-skipping on his cane and observed Lalana's gate, slow and methodical as if she had to think about every step. "Look, I've been out there. I can't let you two get yourselves killed."

"I'm old. I don't know how old, but I've lived seventy-odd years. I'm not afraid of dying."

"But there's no clean water. Nothing to eat. No shelter."

"All the medicines I have, I foraged for. I can spot patterns, striations, the stems that point to essential roots, things you could eat in a pinch that wouldn't twist your bowels into a hard knot." She dug through her bag as if to take inventory.

Sindra thought of the journey, shimmying along the Yarin, fording the canal, the climb down the ladder, the drop at the bottom, the drainage tunnel. "You can't make it."

"You *owe* me."

She spotted a coil of rope and bridle in the stable, envisioning a way to get them down the initial drop in the drainage channel. "Get that rope and some candles. And flint rocks."

Sindra took a deep breath and started back toward the quarantine cellar, explaining to Errol and Lalana the obstacles they would have to overcome and that each of them would have to make it to the hatch by the salvage factory alone—scatter and survive. "I'll do my best to get you down from there."

"Wait," Errol held up his hand. "Something's not right." He disappeared around the stable. Gone for an uncomfortable amount of time, he returned with a worried look on his face. "We're not going anywhere right now. There are ghosts crawling all over Old Town, urgent. Something's going on."

Sindra hunkered in Lalana's stable, ears tuned to the other side of the corral, as the ghost activity in Old Town increased. She could hear them talking, unloading emergency supplies from the make-shift warehouses, and coming sometimes within feet of the stables.

After a tense night of waiting, the curtain of smoke had lifted and hanging in the sky was a discernible disc the color of molten copper, a beautiful sunrise over the mountains, leaving Sindra vulnerable and naked underneath an endless blue.

When Errol returned after another check to see if they had a window of escape, he crouched beside the stable door, a look of panic on his face. "Sindra," he whispered. "Hide." He pushed her toward a bin full of hay. "Hurry."

Sindra burrowed into the hay. Errol covered her feet and any other visible parts as voices sounded from just outside the stable, followed by footsteps and commotion so close to Sindra that she thought they might walk right over her.

"Mule Man," a ghost yelled at Errol. "The Superintendent needs all these mules hitched up to wagons. That donkey, too." He marched around the area where Lalana kept her supplies, motioning for a group of guards to join him.

"Superintendent is mandating firebox material requisition. Take Mule Man and the witch here with you." He pointed to Lalana. "Nobody gets out of this one, gimps, old folks, nobody.

Sindra kept still, holding her breath. Errol hopped passed her to the wall where the tack hung for rigging the wagons. He glanced at her as she peered through strands of hay that blended with her hair, making the top of her head part of the haystack. She waited without moving until the tail of the last mule disappeared from sight. Relieved that Errol and Lalana had left with the ghosts, certain that they would have either gotten her caught, drowned in the canal, or swept away in the drainage tunnel, Sindra emerged from the hay as hungry as she had ever been in her life.

She had seen the mules and horses eating hay. If they ate it, and it made them strong beasts of burden, then she convinced herself that she could it eat, too. Still hidden behind the stable door, she squatted beside the haystack and shoved a handful of hay into her mouth. It pricked her cheeks as she chewed. It had no flavor, and she had a hard time swallowing it. The dry strands wound up into a ball in her mouth as she chewed and chewed, shoving more in and swallowing hard.

The silence in Old Town, after such an active night, reminded Sindra that a better opportunity may never come again. She tucked three candles, a flint rock, and a blanket into a saddle bag and slung it over her shoulder. From corner to corner, keeping in the shadows on the rare sunny day, Sindra made her way through an empty Old Town to an equally vacant Jonesbridge. All the factories, except for munitions #2, sat idle and silent. In the distance, she saw teams, entire shifts, amassing in domicile quadrangles preparing for something she'd never witnessed in Jonesbridge.

With the streets quiet, Sindra ran for the salvage factory keeping low and watchful, invisible, the way she had learned to travel on the rails. When she reached the hatch beside the building, she stepped down onto the ladder, but this time she waited for the flush of drainage from the munitions factory, trying to avoid almost drowning the way she and Myron had. The water rushed beneath her, filled the tunnel below, rising partway up the ladder and then receded. Sindra dropped down and crawled, snaked and groped her way to the canal outtake where she saw hundreds of slogs gathering near the supply depot gates, heads to the sky in wonder at the clear blue heavens, unsure of what they should do next without the protection of the thick smoke overhead.

CHAPTER 13

The sight of the chapel filled Sindra with hope. She approached it with caution and darted for the tunnel hatch near the bell tower. The grate creaked when she inched it open, and digging through the soil, she unearthed Sindra's star, still there, where Myron had buried it for safekeeping.

She hadn't slept last night, her belly groaned for food, and fatigue threatened to overwhelm her. She'd run the entire way through the empty compound, jogged through the shin pines, dodging boulders as though wings had sprouted on her back. Now she had nowhere left to run, no way over the Gorge and no plan. She exhaled and rubbed the star, wiping it clean of dirt.

Sometimes at night, amidst the snoring and grumbling of the rail-walkers, Sindra would lie on her back and gaze at the stars. Out on the rails, in the Nethers, unobstructed by smoke and haze, the stars filled the sky like sprinkles of magnesium dust. For a while she wondered what stars were, how far away they were and how big, but after a time she no longer cared to know. They were real, and they existed somewhere outside the confines of the earth where people could never destroy them. The star Myron had given her was as real as any other because it reminded her, the way real stars did, that the world could never destroy her spirit. Possessing it again, holding it, with the weight of it in her pocket, buoyed her enough to keep going.

With the sky so clear, she headed into the open to soak it all in, the sunlight, the mountains, the dormant factories in the valley. She turned her head straight up, into an endless expanse that—without the smoke and ash to keep her in— she feared she would fall right up into the blue. She spun around, forgetting for a moment where she was when a hand clapped over her mouth from behind. A strong, furry arm yanked her backward toward the chapel, dragging her feet through the dirt.

"Shh," he said in a hoarse whisper. "Don't move."

The odor of his hand made her queasy. It smelled like dead animal, waste, and sulfur all mixed together, and she noticed that when he spoke into her ear that his breath smelled the same. She elbowed him in the ribs. He did not flinch.

"Where's Myron?" Coyote Man removed his hand from her mouth.

"What?" Sindra whispered. "He's gone."

"What do you mean gone? How'd you get here if he didn't bring you?"

"What are you talking about?"

"He wouldn't go over the Gorge without you. Stupid kid. Probably got himself captured."

"Myron isn't stupid." Dread built inside her that she had ever doubted Myron. Sindra jerked free of his grasp. Coyote Man yanked her back.

"All men ensnared by the lure of a woman turn stupid, whether they start off that way or not." He held a finger to his lips. "Quiet. There's a lookout up on Iron's Knob. Can't get to Myron's flying machine from here." He led Sindra down into the creek bed. "Keep low and follow me." He held Sindra by the forearm. His grasp felt like an iron clamp around her arm.

"Where are we going?"

"Someplace *they* don't know about. Keep quiet."

When they reached a stony outcropping, Coyote Man climbed over the bank and waited, motionless. Realizing that now was a risky time to make an escape, Sindra crawled up beside him for a peek. Thirty feet away a ghost holding a pistol sat on a rock.

Coyote Man inched down into the creek bed and adjusted his coyote skins so that the snout and head came up over his head like a hood. He climbed up out of the creek and crawled toward the ghost keeping cover in the rocks.

The ghost fidgeted with the gun, examining it, looking down the barrel and drawing with it in the dirt. He paced and threw rocks at bigger rocks until a flash of fur bashed him over the head with a petrified log. Coyote Man picked up the gun, studied it and tucked it into a bag before he hoisted the ghost up over his shoulder.

"What are you going to do with him?"

"Insurance." Coyote Man hiked toward a knoll a few hundred feet away. "This one's awfully close to my cave."

Sindra followed him through a bramble bush and into a

field of shin pines, watching the ghost's head bobble against Coyote Man's back as they walked.

"Careful. Out here, we're like mice on a salt flat to a hawk."

They crossed over to the other side of the knoll and stopped beside a rusted metal contraption, greenish, halfway protruding from the side of the hill. It had doors with handles and windows. Sindra navigated the rocky embankment and hopped down beside it. "What is that thing?"

"Not sure, but it says here that it's an *oldsmobile*. Guess that's what it is." He pointed to a raised metal word just beneath the trunk and flopped the ghost down beside it. "It's my calaboose now. One thing, though," he said, pulling the pistol out of his bag. "This isn't an ordinary civil guard— this one has license to kill."

"Look at all that metal," Sindra said, examining the oldsmobile, her natural salvage instincts taking over. When Coyote Man popped open the trunk, Sindra put her foot on a rock and climbed up inside, hoping to get a look, wondering if it had a real combustion engine. She gave the rear panel of the trunk a kick until a rusted hole formed.

The front of the oldsmobile was dark and surrounded by earth, but light from the hole behind her lit the space up enough to see a centuries-old mausoleum. Seated behind a steering wheel was a skeleton with a leather hat and a pair of boots in the floorboard, and between the shells of the two seats, Sindra noticed several unrecognizable relics of the past.

She pulled herself all the way in and sat down in the empty seat, as though she were a passenger in a time machine driven by a stylish skeleton, ready to ride away to a long-dead world, a place she could hardly wait to show Myron.

"Get out of there. He's waking up." Coyote Man reached in and tugged on Sindra's smock. As soon as she stepped out, he rolled the ghost into the trunk and slammed the lid.

"You're just going to leave him in there?"

"That depends."

"Let me out," a muffled voice called from inside. The ghost pleaded and banged on the inside of the trunk. "Let me out. Whatever you want. Just let me out of here." The voice underneath the green metal sounded young and scared. Not at all the monster Sindra expected.

Coyote Man slapped the trunk. "Not yet."

Still unsure of her plan to find Myron, Sindra followed Coyote Man to his cave. "We'll rest here as long as we can, but they'll be back. I'll keep first watch." He pointed to the cot.

Exhausted to the point of almost passing out, Sindra could hardly keep her eyes open, but when the odor of the cot struck her, she stretched out on the ground instead and fell asleep within seconds. She dreamt of flying through the air on Myron's airship, only it was the shirker coop, and she plummeted forever into the Gorge, never landing.

She awoke to Coyote Man standing over her, nudging her with his foot. "Get up. Your turn." He plopped down on his cot. "There's a cluster of boulders out that way." He pointed to the south. "A good view from there. Get back and let me know if you see anyone coming."

Sindra struggled to her feet and headed outside. She had seen a few wild people. They lived on the edges, not unlike the rail-walkers, but here in Jonesbridge, such a person as Coyote Man seemed impossible. His ways were strange. He spoke with an inflection in his voice, words with familiar sounds contorted, *winder* instead of *window*. Statements trailed away and then up again like a question.

As she kept her vigil, eying all directions, surprised by how much and how far she could see, a cockroach scurried out into the open across her foot. She took aim, trapped it under her cupped hand and scooped it up. She studied the roach for a moment, upside down on her palm, its legs twitching. Her stomach growled. She closed her eyes and threw it into her mouth, chewing quickly before it moved too much on her tongue. She was relieved that she had rid her body of the black whisper before it worked its dark magic, but what she couldn't feed the life inside her, it would steal from her body.

She had no idea how long she'd kept watch, but the sun had moved halfway across the sky and her thoat burned for water. Her current thirst and hunger could not match the misery of her four-day stint in the shirker coop. That had left a mark on her soul. Without help, she would have died, and she thought of the guard trapped in Coyote Man's make-shift jail. He'd been there a while now. The ghosts had raped her. They'd treated her like property. They'd beaten her and tricked her, but the man in the back of the oldsmobile, an anxious kid like her, would die of thirst the way she almost did in the coop, if she didn't do something. She didn't remember seeing *this* ghost's face, smiling and watching, waiting to drop his pants for a turn, and Errol said that the preacherman he knew told him that good turns have a way of coming around again.

She hurried back to the cave and filled her canteen with water to give him enough to outlast whatever Coyote Man planned to do with him. By the water filter, she spotted three strips of coyote jerky. She bit a chunk off the end. Sinewy and dry, it tasted like the leather strap they used to absorb the pain during the branding tattoo procedure, but it was food, and she would eat anything that would keep the baby inside her growing.

Trekking through the brambles, Sindra spotted the rump of the green oldsmobile jutting out of the side of the ravine like a wart. She had seen these contraptions before, but never one that hadn't completely rusted into a metal skeleton, except for in a museum they came across in an abandoned town on the rails, but that one was much more sleek, faster looking than the one in the ravine, as though it might have flown right out of the museum.

Thoughts of machines like this one kept her awake some nights with visions of a world much different than hers, where calculating computers, so smart they could solve problems, sometimes started their own wars. Sindra had heard all sorts of tales about history, of mechanical people that did the bidding of their creator, and ships that tried to sail to the stars but fell short. Legend told that after a jagged magnetic flash in the sky halted the rhythms of the machines, the Zealots buried the machine carcasses in the ice shelf at the bottom of the world to appease the Great Above. That sounded crazy, yet she couldn't help but imagine what sort of gizmos a real contraptionist could make from a salvage pit like that.

"You still alive in there," Sindra whispered, placing her ear down on the cold metal.

Inside the trunk was silent. She groped for the latch, jiggled it, and pried the lid up. He was alive, shivering, his chest rising and falling as he took in faint sips of air. She placed the extra coyote skin on him. His head jerked back as his eye hinged open. His chattering teeth sounded like a tiny jackhammer.

"Here you are." Sindra put the water to his mouth, letting a stream trickle onto the cracks in his lips. When his mouth opened, she poured more in. "Here's a bite of goat fox." She sat one of the jerky strips and the water beside him and shut the trunk lid.

"No, please. You gotta let me out of here. I won't tell them where you are. Just let me out of here."

"I can't do that."

"Wait," he called. "I know you—*Sindra*, right?"

She cracked open the trunk lid a little to hear him better. "You better not know me the way I—"

"No, I mean, I know what they do to you. It's wrong. I know it's wrong. And you're such, well—" His cheeks turned a shade of pink.

"Go on," Sindra said, skeptical of his sincerity and shut the trunk again.

"Look, I would stop them if I could. Believe me. But I'm powerless. Just like you. I do my job. I live in the domiciles. You're lucky to be in Industry. At least you get to make things."

Sindra had never considered herself lucky, *never*, until she met Myron. "I don't care if you do know it's wrong, you still owe me for watching those devils ravage me like a roadside carpie."

"They conscripted me from a small militia commune. I had a sister and a mother. I'd die before anyone did that to them. Come on. That wild man's going to kill me."

Sindra thought for a minute. If Myron had gone to Jonesbridge for her and hadn't returned, that meant he got caught. "Where's the other fugitive?"

"Another guard's going to relieve me of duty out here soon. More are coming."

"Where's the other fugitive? Tall, black hair."

After a few moments he responded. "They took him to the coop."

The lasting image of an eerily empty Jonesbridge made the thought of the coop even more dire. No smoke, no factories, no people, which meant no one like Errol, no one at all with water or blankets. Sindra leaned over and threw up, morning sickness or anxiety, she couldn't tell which. Both sensations turned her stomach upside down.

"Look, that wild man has your gun. There's no getting it back. But I might let you out of here—for a price." The ghost in the trunk did seem to have what the old-timers called apology in his voice. Anyone could muster the proper words to say *sorry,* but someone who meant it had a tension in the voice, almost like a taut guitar string.

"What? Anything."

"If I let you out of there, the first thing you do is go to the coop and let Myron out."

"I can't go back until the next guard relieves me. They'll kill me."

"Stay here and the wild man will kill you with your own gun, or you can die in this trunk. Besides, the whole compound is empty. Shouldn't be too hard. You owe me."

"Okay. I promise. I'll do it. Just open this up. I can't take closed-in places."

Sindra tripped the trunk latch.

"Th-thanks." The ghost climbed out, keeping an eye on her.

As he turned away in the direction of the compound, Sindra grabbed him by the collar on his orange shirt and whipped him around to face her. "What's the first thing you're going to do?" When he didn't answer, she slapped him across the face, a blow hard enough to make her hand sting. "First thing?"

"Shirker coop."

She held him facing her until he said it again.

"Straight there to let him out."

Sindra leaned against the car to catch her breath. "Tell him to meet me at the chapel."

In his hurry to escape the trunk, the ghost left the canteen of water Sindra had brought him. She tucked it into the saddle bag with the candles and headed up to the top of the knoll, which gave her a panoramic view of the valley. She witnessed waves of tiny gray figures pouring out of the compound, scores of her fellow slogs spreading out into the countryside, some behind the mule-drawn carts, others in large groups, painting the barren landscape slog-smock gray. It looked like hundreds, maybe a thousand.

Unexpected noises greeted her as she neared the chapel, voices, the sounds of saws and heavy hammers. She crept into the shadow of the creek bank and followed the steep embankment to the bend where countless feet shuffled through the brush. Sindra got a handhold in the soft bank and pulled up until she could see the chapel. Slogs, ghosts, foremen, at least a hundred, in, around, and all over the chapel ripped it apart board by board and pulled up or cut every shin pine sprig that dared to pierce the soil.

Now gone completely, sky had replaced the sagging roof of the chapel, and the crew had turned their attention to the walls. Some boards splintered off in shards. Others took the force of the hundred-slog destruction team to work off, prying and pulling until the wood moaned before the walls finally came to rest in a flurry of dust that left only a waist-high stone foundation in the shape of a chapel. Watching this process, Sindra felt as though they had ripped her apart as well.

On the far side of the chapel, near where the bell tower once stood, Sindra spotted a mule-drawn cart with Lalana and Errol adjusting the load as slogs piled on boards and sticks and anything else that would burn. She slid down the bank, kneeling as low as she could, envisioning the spring thaw that would bring a toxic wash through the gulley.

"Hey, what are you doing?"

Sindra looked up to see a ghost, discipline rod drawn, standing at the edge of the creek.

"Got a deserter." He motioned for another ghost to join him.

The other ghost reached down and grabbed Sindra by the hair, pulling her to her feet and up off the ground. She twisted in midair by her hair until she flopped out on the ground at the feet of two ghosts.

CHAPTER 14

Myron pulled at the bars on the coop, rattled them, rammed his back into the door until he collapsed against the web of cold metal, now certain he was going to die. His vision was blurry. He saw two of each of the bars on the cage, six smokestacks over munitions instead of three, two of everything. His mouth felt like it was lined with burlap, and he couldn't swallow. Just one sip, that's all he needed, a single drop of water.

If not for the munitions factory still in operation, Jonesbridge would resemble one of the extinct towns on the rails Sindra described. Myron's ears had grown so accustomed to the hum of factory turbines that their absence made his head ache. In the corner of his eye, he spotted movement, giving him hope that someone would bring him water. On the backside of Munitions #2, a man crawled along the ground pushing a roll of wire. He adjusted it every few feet, pushing the wire to the edge of the building. Myron rubbed his eyes, trying to focus, convincing himself he was not hallucinating.

The man wasn't wearing the gray burlap of a slog, or the orange of Civility, but administrator tan. His face blurred in and out of focus, but Myron recognized him, Cyril, the salvage factory administrator. The man stopped to attach a brown bundle to the wire, continued and stopped again, repeating this until he reached the corner of the building. After checking in all directions, Cyril assembled a black tripod with a box on top that was a little bigger than a ration crate. From a bag, he pulled out a set of salvage tools and attached the wire in several places to the black box. He tinkered with it, turned his wrench, checked over his shoulder and adjusted it some more, never noticing that someone was in the coop—watching.

Myron dangled his arm through the cage, resting his head on the door hinge. His mouth felt as though he had eaten sand. First he saw the white sand of Bora Bora, but that gave way to the dunes of a far away desert, a place his Old Age atlas called Sahara, where a waterless ocean of sand drifted with the wind, and when the sun fell, the parched ground grew cold. Sahara, he thought would make a lovely name for a girl.

"You Myron?"

Myron lifted his head, unsure if the voice was real.

"Hurry." The shirker coop lowered to the ground. It wasn't the salavage administrator he'd seen earlier outside Munitions, but someone different, a man in orange, a ghost, that unlocked the cage door and inched it open.

Myron crawled out of the coop. His legs cramped and his bones ached. When he spotted the canal his thirst took over, certain that if he didn't get a drink in the next few seconds the coop would have beaten him. He didn't care why or who had opened the door—water, that was all. Knees scraping the brick walkway, he pulled himself toward the canal as the liquid shimmered in the sunlight, taunting him. When he reached the edge of the water, he dug both hands in to scoop a drink. The water dripped through his fingers as he raised it to his mouth.

"No!" The ghost that had freed Myron ran up behind him and rolled him over, slapping Myron's hands from his mouth. "Don't do it. That stuff will kill you."

"I'm so thirsty." Myron sprawled out on the ground, still disoriented.

The ghost opened his canteen and gave Myron a swig. "Sindra set me free. So I'm setting you free. She's out there." He pointed in the direction of Iron's Knob. "Said to meet her somewhere—a chapel I think. Don't know what that means, but you're on your own, now." The ghost wrenched his canteen from Myron's lips and jogged toward the Civil Guard post.

"Sindra?" Myron stumbled to his feet, heading toward the salvage factory and the grate.

The factories, all red brick, were otherwise covered in windows so that they required no artificial light during the daytime hours. From inside the factories, especially the administrator's office or the foreman's perch, only the haze in the air and other factories obstructed the view. As he passed Munitions #2, he remembered that there were at least two hundred slogs still hard at work in munitions with an administrator on duty and two ghosts at the door, so he snaked along the ground to keep under the line of windows.

When he got closer, he spotted the tripod, the black box, and the empty spool of wire that the salvage administrator had set around the factory, wondering what he had been doing and why. Still crawling, Myron followed the wire to the first bundle, which he recognized as mining ordinance, rock blaster they called it. Affixed to the bundle of explosives was a wire mechanism that looked like a mouse trap. Myron continued along the wire to the next bundle, the same as the last, following it until he reached the tripod.

Connectors, wires, incongruent devices hemmed together, all topped by an antenna; this stuff had to have come from the salvage floor. This surprised him because the law forbade anyone, even the administrator of the factory in question, from taking anything from a factory. An ornate clock, something Myron recognized, a piece he had processed himself, sat beside the antenna. The hands on the clock did not move.

From the box, another larger wire ran across the brick pathway to the edge of Munitions #1, currently shut down due to coal shortage. From there, another wire ran to Ironworks. It was an explosive chain, some sort of a bomb, and a big one. Myron studied the jumble of connectors and yanked out the one leading across the path. A mechanism under the clock clicked. The clicks grew louder and more frequent with each until a thud sounded inside the box, and the hands on the clock began to move. Myron looked back along the wall at the spacing of the explosives, placed at support beams, and thought of the many slogs that worked day shift at Munitions #2.

Munitions employed Jonesbridge's most productive, most patriotic, and trusted workers. He knew a couple of them. They had transferred there after exemplary performance in Salvage.

Myron pulled another wire that connected the clock to the mechanism below it, hoping that would stop the device. The clock ticked faster, as though time had sped up. The antenna, like Coyote Man's radio, Myron knew could receive a signal through the air, so he yanked it off and broke it in half. Another device snapped, and the clock's second hand sped around the face. It reminded him of the time he pulled a board from under a contraption in his grandfather's barn, and the whole thing fell apart with a crash.

The ticking continued to speed up. Myron had run out of ideas to stop the process. He panicked and jumped up, peeking through the glass of the nearest window at all the slogs inside.

Myron ran along the back of the munitions factory, tempted to slap on the windows, yelling *bomb*, urging his fellow slogs to flee for cover. They had to get out of there, but Myron had just escaped the coop. He had to find Sindra. They had a plan.

He sprinted toward the canal, but the ghost at the entrance of Munitions #2 saw him.

"The shirker's loose!" the ghost yelled, pointing to the empty shirker coop. He grabbed two other ghosts and hurried in Myron's direction with their discipline rods raised.

Myron stopped. He turned around slowly with his hands in the air. "There is a bomb. Goes all the way around Munitions #2. You have to go back and get everybody out." Myron enunciated each word with care.

The ghosts froze, stopping their chase for the moment. One ghost turned to the others and nodded. "There's a what?"

"A bomb."

"What? Not satisfied with shirking. You want to take everybody out with you?"

"No. No. I didn't do it. I saw it." Myron shook his head, the urgent tick of the bomb clock playing in his head. "No! You got it wrong."

"Bomb!" A ghost yelled. He headed toward Munitions #2. The other two ran toward Myron.

"The shirker's loose," a ghost yelled. He chased Myron down the brick path between factories.

His legs still cramping from dehydration, Myron slipped behind the outtake of Munitions #1. The two ghosts ran passed. He trained his eye on the doors of Munitions #2, expecting, hoping, praying to see hundreds of his fellow slogs pouring out to safety, but he only saw the foreman standing out front, surveying the situation.

"There he is." The two ghosts ran towards him. Myron headed for the canal bridge. On the other side he could make it to Salvage and the grate where he could escape. He spotted a courier bicycle leaning against a coal shed. He hopped on and pedaled. His legs burned.

As he reached the bridge, he tumbled off the bicycle when the ground underneath him shook, the earth slipping from under the wheels. An explosion rocked the building behind him, a deafening blast as if it had filled his ears with wet clay. He steadied himself on the bridge wall, and caught in the murky reflection of the Yarin Canal, window after window popping out of Munitions #2 with each successive blast, all two hundred slogs unable to escape in time.

In Jonesbridge, slogs had more in common with

overloaders and copper ore and salvage material than people. They represented production, pieces processed, ore smelted, steel refined—take a slog away, subtract the numbers. Munitions #2, where they combined the saltpeter, charcoal, and sulfur to fabricate black powder, where they assembled the ammunition, the artillery shells, piss whistles, and bullets, each one of those mattered, and as the fire spread, the chain reaction of explosions ended in thunder that rattled Myron's teeth.

He raced across the bridge, leaping into the noxious waters of the Yarin ahead of the hot blast and flurry of broken glass, dust and ash that rocketed across the water. Bricks and debris rained onto Myron as he struggled to keep his head up while avoiding the fallout. Beside him, the shirker coop splashed down followed by the chain that it had hung on. The water sloshed, and a wave rose from the base of the demolished factory, sending Myron down the Yarin so fast he couldn't get to the bank.

He treaded water and fought to navigate a barrage of sharp metal and bricks as the rainstorm of detritus continued. He hoisted his arms over a door floating beside him and rode the Yarin until he could see a plume of black smoke darkening the sky above Jonesbridge, mournful of the sudden loss of two hundred of his fellow slogs who hadn't been able to escape. Some ghosts ran for cover, but others gave chase, certain Myron was to blame for the mayhem. They jumped into a coal barge tug and pursued Myron on the turbulent canal.

Beginning with stinging on his legs, the canal water started to burn. Myron crawled farther onto the door, paddling toward the bank, which was a steep wall of concrete on either side in this part of the canal. Where the water disappeared on the horizon in front of him, he saw only sky and remembered that the final destination for the Yarin was the bottom of the Great Gorge.

Behind him, the boat filled with ghosts gained on him. Myron paddled to the concrete wall. A gun fired. The bullet ricocheted across the canal, striking the door inches away from his chest. The current in the canal continued to race him toward the Gorge lock. He paddled to the bank, worked all the way on top of the door and steadied himself with his hands along the wall, the stone scraping his palms as he got up to his knees. The door tipped underneath him. He regained his balance, leaning against the wall, and in one sudden movement, rose to his feet and reached for the top of the wall. As he dangled from the ledge, the door sped off down the canal without him while the ghosts upstream got closer.

Myron hoisted himself over the bank and rolled down the levy where he scrambled to a control platform. There he witnessed the salvage administrator turning a red valve. Myron's eyes met the man's who had just killed two hundred of his fellow slogs.

Just as he decided to stop the salvage administrator from doing more harm, behind him, the top of a ladder hooked over the wall from the canal. The ghosts from the tug in the canal had caught up with him, and the real bomber stood right in front of him, someone he could never accuse because an administrator's word would always carry more weight than a slog's. Unsure of his bearings, Myron ran in the opposite direction of the plume of black smoke rising from Munitions #2. The salvage administrator also ran, but in the other direction.

With all the craziness occuring, he thought,—if he could find Sindra—they might make it over the Gorge after all. He fled toward the chapel with abandon, no looking over his shoulder, no keeping out of sight, in a sprint to stay ahead of the ghosts he had managed to evade—and the column of smoke rising from Munitions #2.

Myron reached the chapel to a chaotic scene. A hundred slogs and nearly as many ghosts had convened in the footprint of what was once the chapel. Some were staring at the smoke from the demolished factory, others hung their heads as the ghosts tried to regain order.

Myron's grandfather once told him that what we were was a big part of who we are, that old discarded buildings, like old discarded people, have something to say. Myron had listened to the decaying chapel. He had heard what it told him about how people used to live, and he had heard his grandfather's advice from inside the walls, a voice now dismantled board by board and loaded on mule carts to feed the bellies of war factories. Seeing it all gone evoked the pain of losing his grandfather, but in that pain he could find his strength.

In the middle of the fray, Myron spotted Sindra. Surrounded by ghosts, she kicked one direction and punched in another. One ghost had her by the hair. The other swung at her with his discipline rod. He had seen enough today. Myron stood from his hiding position and charged the ghosts from behind, his anger manifesting in the form a shrill coyote howl, envisioning what they had done to her late at night, and in front of him, and what they continued to do.

Myron grabbed the unsuspecting ghost's discipline rod

and whacked him across the back of his head. The others scattered. He could see Sindra's smile emerge under her hair that resembled a pitchfork full of hay hanging down over her face. Their eyes locked. She wiped her hair from her face. He had hoped the next time he looked into her eyes it would remind him that everything would somehow turn out. Instead, he saw fear—that this moment might be the last time their eyes would ever meet.

Myron ducked a punch and swung at the nearest ghost, landing a hit in his abdomen. Sindra jumped on his back and rode him to the ground. Myron swung again in a broad sweep, connecting with arms and heads at random as the other ghosts ran toward him. He heard the clap of gunfire. Everyone froze as the ghost next to Myron fell to the ground. Another clap followed, this time from the creek bed, ending in a flurry of dust.

Several ghosts blew their whistles at once. Myron looked up to see a team of four mules pulling an armored combat tank on track wheels, pieced together by parts of different machines, all topped off with a cannon turret. It stopped on the other side of the creek. Two defensemen sat beneath the barrel of the cannon as it spun in the direction just beyond the chapel where the gunfire originated. A whoosh of air passed over Myron's face. He jerked his head in the direction of the whistling projectile to see it impact the hillside behind him with an explosion. Clumps of dirt and rocks rained down.

Myron spotted Coyote Man with a pistol in his hand hiding in the creek. When the ghost leader took aim on Coyote Man, Myron rushed him, striking his head with a discipline rod. More shots sounded from the opposite direction. Myron turned toward the other guards, and, in that moment, another pop that ended in a thump, connected with the meat of Myron's thigh. It felt like the time he snagged his leg on a jagged piece of scrap iron, a deep penetrating hit that cut and bruised at the same time. Everything inside his body quickened, his heart, breathing, thoughts racing about what he wished he and Sindra could have done together.

Myron grabbed his leg and tumbled over in time to see dozens of confused slogs in a jumble, some hiding on the ground, some just standing there, looking at him. Others came to his aid. An older man about Coyote Man's age stood over him, gawking at him. Myron handed him the rod, and the man eyed it as though he knew he should have a spirit somewhere inside that transcended that of a common slog. He shook the rod and began swinging blindly right up the gut of an approaching squad of ghosts, yelling, taking one swat after another.

Myron watched as his fellow slogs, people he had never met, jumped into the skirmish, flailing, punching and swinging boards, but they all fell, one by one, each after the dull pop of one of the ghost's guns. The base of the old chapel soon filled with lifeless bodies.

Myron could feel the blood gushing out of him like the muck churning through the turbines in the Yarin Canal. He felt lighter, his thoughts leaving him. He crawled toward the ravine. With bullets whizzing by, people dying, chaos all around, he imagined being at the front lines, about to die the same way his father had, and it made him realize how secure life in Jonesbridge was, where he had at least been alive enough to dream.

The closer he got to the safety of the dry creek bank,

Myron felt as though his body was bubbling down the drain on the salvage floor in a vortex of sanitizer, that he was a float making one desperate bob after another to surface. He could hear the holler of guards mustering aid from other teams on their way to the scene. And in the first clear blue sky in years, between the firearms exchanging pops and the cries of scattering slogs and ghosts, Myron heard muffled thunder—a motor.

Above him, a sight he'd dreamed of his entire life, a bi-wing flying airplane, just like the ones in his grandfather's books, sputtered across the sky ahead of a trail of popping black smoke.

The propeller puttered, spinning sporadically, threatening to stop. The airplane carried two passengers, one in front of the other, the pilot and a man dropping piss whistles from saddlebags that draped over the fuselage.

The world closed in on Myron as he watched. The sounds rumbled as the barren mountains acted as drumheads for a giant performance of the morning anthem. It drew nearer, thunderous echoes, pounding from the south and the east, the rattling boom of an overloader track in quick repetition, so close now he expected the wheels to roll right over him. He reached out his hand for Sindra and Coyote Man to pull him down. The ground beneath him shook after another zoomed across the sky, and again, rocking the ground.

The chaos at the chapel ended suddenly with the explosions, as every man or woman left standing turned in the direction of the blasts in time to see the bi-wing airplane crash right into the Ironworks, now the tallest smokestack in Jonesbridge after Munitions #2 had gone down. The factory beneath the stack exploded into an orange ball of successive percussions until it disappeared completely into a puff of dust.

"The E'sters are here!"

"Run for the mines!" A stampede of slogs and ghosts alike took off down the hill in the opposite direction of the factories on their way to the mines.

"The E'sters are—" another voice yelled, this time a ghost. His warning was cut short by the blast of a piss whistle ten feet away.

Following another explosion, this one closer, Coyote Man managed to pull Myron down into the ravine.

Myron tried to bring his hand to Sindra's face as the fuzzy edges of the world closed in around her. He concentrated on a vision, the setting sun as it fell between two palm trees in Bora Bora, sand still warm from the day, with white, yellow, and blue birds riding the ocean breeze, whistling sounds all around him. But he could feel the blood leaving his body, his life slipping away the way his mom's had, and in the cluster of faces around him now, he searched for his mother's to lead him to the Great Above.

CHAPTER 15

"Open up in there." The muffled calls, two of them, came from outside the front door. Shadows crawled across the counter when Myron's mom shut the kitchen shutters.

Myron knew what to do. He hurried to the potato bin, which stank of mildew and soil. The bin door snapped closed. His knees pushed up against his nose. He could hardly breathe. His mom claimed that a six-year-old boy could fit anywhere, as though he were a shirt that she could fold over mid-chest and place in a drawer.

"Look," the deepest of the voices called, tapping on the kitchen shutter, "We saw you go in the house. If I have to bust the door down, you better be dead. Now open up."

Myron eased open the potato bin door for a look into the kitchen to see his mom straighten her apron and march toward the front door. He'd seen that look on her face before, always just after he'd done something wrong, and once she had that look, the only way to change her expression was for

Myron to do as he was told.

A robe filled his view, his grandfather's hairy legs, and then the door to the bin slammed shut to darkness, soil and spiders of all kinds. The front door clicked. Voices in the other room sounded as though they came from underneath a wet blanket. The men stomped through the house clanging and shouting. His mother started to cry. Myron breathed faster. His heart quickened. It felt like the time he fell into the mill pond before he knew how to swim, when his insides filled up with water, and his mother had to jump in, all her clothes on, and yank him out by his arms.

The clamor grew closer until they reached the kitchen. "I told you," his mother screamed. "They already came for him!"

"Then you won't mind if we have a look around."

"That's not necessary," Myron's grandfather explained. "We are law-abiding citizens."

Myron figured his grandfather didn't want them to go into the barn, that they might see all the stuff he worked on out there, gadgets and machines they would confiscate.

"Well, then, as law-abiding citizens, you won't have any problems."

Cabinet doors in the kitchen creaked open and closed. Drawers jerked in and out. The stomp of their shoes on the floor grew closer, echoing from the hallway and back to the kitchen again. Myron couldn't hold back his tears when he heard his mother sob. The tears ran down his cheeks, but as cramped as he was, he couldn't wipe them away. He could only sniff as they dripped off the end of his nose.

Light stung Myron's eyes when the potato bin door flung open. Two men in orange uniforms, the color of the

Civility Administration, came into focus. "There you are," the larger of the two men said.

"I thought I smelled something," the other one chimed in.

"Don't touch him. Don't touch my baby, you animals." Myron's mom still wore her look of determination. She jumped in front of the cabinet door between Myron and the two men.

"Ma'am, we have been through this with you on three occasions. The first time we came, we were quite cordial. Weren't we?" He turned to his partner, swatting him on the chest. "Then, we came with the necessary paperwork. Now, we're done. This is it."

"Mrs. Daw," the larger of the two men read from a clipboard. He gave her a stern glare. "What would happen if you were, I don't know, sitting around playing winky twiddle or some such—with your boy here—and an E'ster piss whistle shot right through your window? Boom! Everyone kaput." He slammed his hand flat on the kitchen table.

"Now, imagine that happening, which it does every day, and responsible people, such as yourself, did not take the necessary steps to protect their children," the other man added.

Myron heard their voices, but his mother's body blocked his view. "Mom, I don't want to go," he yelled. He squirmed out of the potato pantry, parting his mother's legs like a curtain, darting through them, right into the hands of the two men he hoped to escape.

"Now we got you."

"No one can protect him like I can," his mother screamed.

"Exactly. Which is why the Superintendent of Civility has ordered that all children be taken into protective custody. All children. That means this little rat, too."

"To ensure the survival of our people, ma'am."

"By enslaving them?"

"He's got to be good for something. We all have to do our part."

The tall man clamped his hands around Myron's wrists while his mom grabbed his legs. The pull from both ends made him feel like a piece of festival taffy. When his grandfather jumped in to help, Myron's mom let go of his feet and grabbed the vegetable hatchet from the kitchen sink.

"Nora, no," Myron's grandfather screamed. He reached out to stop her, but the hatchet had already hit its mark, buried in the man's forehead as though it were a ripe turnip.

"You're not taking my baby. You hear me?"

The grip around Myron's wrists loosened. Myron fell to the floor with a thud, so frightened he had stopped crying, his tears frozen on his cheeks.

"Run, Myron, run," his mother urged.

He did. He ran for an hour until he finally collapsed at the edge of the abandoned quarry. He wondered if his mother killed the man, and then his worries turned to what the other one might do, what his grandfather would do, and what might happen to them. The moment he caught his breath, Myron hopped up and ran back the way he came, crying the entire way, his stomach tight and his head spinning. When he topped the hill next to the family barn, he saw his grandfather tugging the bodies of the two orange shirts, stripped down to their skivvies and soaked in red, into the barn.

Myron reached his grandfather just as the barn door

swung shut. His grandfather knelt down beside the men, now powerless with the orange color of Civility having been stripped from their backs. "What does that say?" Myron asked as he watched his grandfather placing signs around their necks.

"It says *deserter*. Dishonoring them is the only way. This is bad, Myron. Very bad. You're too young to understand, but I have no choice."

Myron remembered seeing people along the road from Billingston with similar signs the year before. They were people who ran away from their responsibility, from the war, when they were supposed to fight. They'd been made examples of, his grandfather had told him. The whole scene made him sick. He wanted his mother.

"Where's mom?"

"No, Myron. No," his grandfather whispered with his head down. "You have to be strong. As strong as a boy your age can possibly be."

Myron rushed up to the porch before his grandfather could stop him. "Mom," he yelled when he saw the blanket, hands sticking out from either side, a trail of blood leading from the kitchen to the porch. As much as he had wanted his mother to be hiding from him, like she did when they played search-and-find, she hadn't come out when he called *overs*. That was their code word for when Myron got scared that he couldn't find his mom, and she would jump out of hiding and give him a hug. He pulled back the blanket. He saw her there, not moving, not blinking, lifeless, the vegetable hatchet sticking out of the side of her head, and he was sure he would never want to play another game the rest of his life.

His grandfather tugged the blanket over her body and hugged him.

"Why didn't you save her?" Myron cried.

His grandfather's jaw bulged. "It should be me under that blanket, Myron."

Later that day, after they buried Myron's mother, his grandfather dragged the slain Civil Guards, now labeled as deserters, beside the road to Richterville. "This will buy us some time."

"What happens if they come back looking for me again?"

His grandfather led him to the fresh grave where they'd buried his mom and grabbed a shovel. "This one will be yours, Myron." He broke ground and tossed the shovelful of dirt aside.

"What?" Myron watched as a second grave took shape next to his mother's.

"If they come back—you died with your mom." His grandfather pointed to the second, smaller patch of raised, fresh earth.

•   •   •

"You have to save him," Sindra yelled.

Myron opened his eyes. His vision blurred. Voices and faces mixed into a collage of activity. "I'm an animal doctor. Does this look like a mule?" Lalana spat into her hands and rubbed the pendent around her neck with her moistened fingers before she closed her eyes and lowered her head.

"What's she doing? How will that help?" Sindra yelled.

"She's summoning her Custodian," Errol whispered. "She always does that in medical emergencies."

Myron blinked in and out of consciousness, picturing Ortheo, the horned owl. Each species of animal once had its own spirit Custodian. When a type of animal vanished forever from the earth, so too did its Custodian. Now, as Myron understood it, there were so few animals that all the animals remaining had only one to share.

Lalana leaned down, putting her finger on Myron's neck. "He's still with us. Barely. A mess of this donkey hide gelatin and a bit of mugwort leaf ought to slow the bleeding—for now. Don't have much of either."

Several explosions pounded the ground just outside the ravine. Lalana pulled a burlap strip around Myron's leg and tied it into a knot, her face crinkling with effort. She did the same with the other, right on top of the wound. The strips of burlap pinked immediately, but within a few seconds, the bleeding stopped.

"I don't know how long he'll last with that metal cap in his leg—" Another blast in the distance stopped Lalana mid-sentence. "Struck a bleeder."

"Bunker," Myron mumbled, unsure if he'd actually said the words or thought them. "Halfway up Iron's Knob."

"That'll be tricky." Coyote Man scanned the ground for fallen ghosts and picked up an extra gun. He fiddled with it until the cylinder opened, checking for bullets just as an artillery shell whistled overhead, exploding midway up Iron's Knob. One of the mules, still harnessed to a wagon, brayed as dirt and stones rained down on him. The mule kicked, extending its neck, trying to break free from the wagon, his distressed call sounding like the horn on a coal barge.

Myron slipped in and out of awareness, but when they lifted him up out of the creek bed, rolling him like a log to a flat spot of earth, his pain brought the world into focus.

"Get that wagon," Lalana pointed to the mule.

Errol calmed the mule and led him toward Myron. With the mule standing beside him, Myron could see blood oozing from a hole in its belly and the hide on his haunches scraped, droplets of blood glistening in the sunlight. Sindra hopped into the wagon and tossed the sharp pieces of wood and shin pines out, clearing a spot for Myron. Coyote Man lifted him into the wagon with what remained of the debris poking into his back.

Lalana inspected the mule's injuries, clicking her tongue several times, shaking her head as she rummaged through her medicine bag. "It's all right, Surrey." She held her hand beneath his nostrils and stroked his mane. "Surrey's my best mule. Strong enough to outpull a steam cart at full throttle." She knelt down and stared at the wound in his belly. "Come on, boy." She climbed on the wagon and grabbed the reins.

The cart rolled through a rut and continued up the hillside, switch-backing up Iron's Knob. Myron rocked with the sway of the wagon. He gazed into the endless blue sky, dreaming of Sindra, unsure whether he was awake or asleep. When he noticed an unusual rock that resembled a giant gear, something Myron used as a landmark to get to the bunker, he knew they were getting close.

Explosions rocked the ground around them. The wagon tilted. Surrey brayed and moaned. Myron rolled to the other side of the wagon and toppled out as it tipped completely. The wood and debris in the wagon cascaded over him, followed by Sindra and Errol who tumbled out ahead of the crashing wagon. Surrey plopped down, rolling to his side, braying.

Hearing Surrey, his agony, reminded Myron of his own pain. Lying in the pile of wood, Myron couldn't move. His chest tightened, his breathing grew labored.

"Wildman, give me that pistol." Lalana spat in her hands and rubbed the pendent around her neck. She grabbed Coyote Man's gun, cocked the hammer, and fired one shot between Surrey's eyes. "Best mule I've ever known. You deserved better than what you got." She closed her eyes and turned around.

Conducting a frantic search of the firebox material that came out of the wagon, Sindra found a long board that could function as a litter, sturdy enough to tie Myron to and get him the rest of the way to the bunker. At first, Sindra lifted the board up by Myron's feet, the lighter end. His head swelled and he blacked out for a moment.

"Turn that man around," Lalana shouted.

Sindra struggled to lift the other end, only able to do so with Coyote Man's help. Now feet down, head up, Myron ascended Iron's Knob on a board that felt as though it might splinter any moment, thumping off rocks as they took turns dragging it, until Coyote Man stopped and stomped his foot on the ground. "This is it."

A thin rectangular opening, a turret vent, spanned a rock face. Inside the rock was a reinforced concrete bunker from a war long past where soldiers protected their high ground, safe from everything but heavy ordinance. Sindra gave Myron's litter one last tug and set it down, gazing down a narrow set of steps that led to a jumble of fabric and strange wooden pieces.

Myron moaned, tugging at the restraints on the board, almost rolling off of it completely. "The airship. Is everything there?"

"I don't know," Sindra said. Her eyes widened as she looked at all the pieces.

"Be careful. It all has to fit together," Myron whispered.

"Listen to all that artillery. Even *if*, and that's a big *if*, this thing takes flight, we'll be a giant target floating through the air," Coyote Man said. He, Errol and Sindra formed a line on the stairs to shuttle all the pieces of Myron's flying contraption out of the bunker.

Myron conceded the added danger, but he'd rather fall out of the sky than wait for a horde of E'sters to storm the gate. "I have to build it." He grew dizzy as he spoke. "Need help with it."

Seeing so many hands on the parts to his airship, all the activity around his creation that he'd fought for piece by piece gave Myron sudden nervous energy that faded as quickly as it arrived. He tried to speak, tried to lift his head, but gravity yanked it back to earth as if his head had been attached to a rope.

Another shell zoomed above them, this one closer. The impact caused a rock slide on the cliff side of Iron's Knob. Stones large and small thundered down, sliding through a cloud of dust that rose from the base of the hill.

"Take cover." Coyote Man motioned to the bunker.

From inside the dust cloud, a gun shot rang through the air. A spray of dirt sprouted between Errol and Coyote Man. They all looked in the direction of the pistol report to see a man standing on the edge of the creek.

As the figure came into view, Myron was shocked to see that it was the salvage administrator, standing there with a gun in his hand. Myron's imagination carried him to the inevitable end, his airship being destroyed, Sindra being killed, his dreams washed away at the hands of a leader—an administrator—a traitor, already responsible for the deaths of hundreds of his fellow slogs. But Myron couldn't move or talk, and the sun had transformed into a flat disk of yellow with everything around it dark. He'd lost so much blood. His leg burned and a sudden wave of cold air rushed through him as though the winter wind blew inside of him, and even the sounds around him slipped away.

CHAPTER 16

"Ramani!" the salvage factory administrator called from the hillside. "Damn it all, that is you under all that fur." He strode over to Coyote Man to embrace him. "Soon as I heard about a wildman, I knew you'd survived. Listen to those bombs. We did it. We actually did it."

Witnessing this exchange between Coyote Man and the salvage administrator siphoned away Sindra's remaining hope. She leaned over Myron and placed her ear over his mouth relieved to hear him breathing, as faint as it was. She stared at him, memorizing every feature of his face in case she would have to someday tell the child she carried about the man who fueled her dreams.

"Ramani didn't survive, Cyril. That man is gone. I've transformed."

"Tranformed?" Cyril gave Coyote Man a firm pat on the back. "This noxious air has really gotten to you." He laughed. "Time for these hill monkeys to get what's coming to them."

Sindra had heard many stories of the enemy. Aside from fighting under another banner, the E'sters had a divergent set of values from what her people had. She'd never seen one herself, but if the salvage factory administrator was an E'ster spy, *anyone* could be. If they didn't look different from her, or speak another tongue, how could anyone determine an enemy from a countryman? One thing she knew for certain was whoever, or whatever, the E'sters were, once they made it across the bridge, they would show no mercy of any kind. Sindra realized then that they couldn't stay here and wait for the carnage. They had to go now. She formulated one plan after another, but all her plans involved running, and in his current state, that meant leaving Myron, her dreams, everything that mattered. When she considered staying and fighting, in her mind, it always ended with Myron dying.

Her planning ended suddenly when Cyril pointed his pistol, first at Errol, before changing his sights to Lalana until his aim finally landed on Sindra. A smile grew on his face. Sindra stared down the barrel of the gun in Cyril's hand as though she were looking into the eyes of the first ghost that had ever raped her. She kept her eye on the muzzle, mesmerized, wondering how such a tiny hole could cause so much fear, so much damage.

"Me and Ramani need a trophy. *You* are coming with us." Cyril grabbed Sindra by the hair, shoving the barrel of his gun into her back. "But since I am a generous man, I'll give the rest of you gimps to the count of three to be out of my sight, or I'll give you a bullet." He pulled Sindra close, tying her arms together behind her back with the straps from Myron's litter.

"Don't waste a bullet on a slog. We need all the ammo we can get." Coyote Man stepped in front of him. "Let's go."

Cyril laughed. "Don't tell me you've taken to these hill monkeys."

Sindra watched Coyote Man's face as Cyril spoke, unable to tell if he'd truly transformed into a coyote, a neutral party in the wild, or whether Cyril had awakened some part of the old *Ramani* along with his E'ster allegiances.

With a shove to her back, Cyril followed Sindra as they left the bunker and Myron behind. Her hands were cinched so tightly behind her that her shoulders ached, and the cold gun barrel nestled at the base of her back reminded her of how difficult escaping would be. It would do Myron no good at all for her to find the same fate as his, so she stumbled along ahead of Cyril, the E'ster pig, as they climbed through the creek bed, listening to him yammer about his triumphs as a recon in the old country and their perilous trek all the way from Chesapeake to Jonesbridge, sniffing out all the decoys along the way.

"That your handiwork?" Coyote Man asked, nodding at the smoldering munitions factory down in Jonesbridge.

"That's right."

"How'd you pull that off?"

"It wasn't easy. I've been planning it since you got tossed on the dead heap. Almost got caught a time or two." He whistled. "A civil guard saw me smuggling the last bit. I took care of him and everything else went as planned. Soon as the coal stopped coming I knew our brothers had found us."

With constant prodding, they made quick time over rocks and up the hill, passing bodies along the way, heading to the top of Iron's Knob where they could watch the

E'ster invasion in safety. The sun had begun to set, and the E'sters continued to pepper the countryside with artillery. Coyote Man stopped suddenly. He raised his hand and stood motionless glaring at a spot on the hillside.

Sindra followed his sightline and spotted a coyote with a bent ear standing in the path of the setting sun. Prepared to dart away, the coyote froze in Coyote Man's gaze. "It's Nick," he whispered.

"What?"

Coyote Man flicked his own ear to point out Nick's half ear. He held a finger to his mouth. Dropping to all fours, Coyote Man yipped and howled, a high-pitched wail, never taking his eyes off of the coyote. The coyote's one good ear twitched.

"Come on. We don't have time for this."

When Cyril spoke, the coyote whipped around and trotted across the hillside. Coyote Man's expression soured. A whistling sound passed over head, and another.

Nick ran right into the path of an E'ster piss whistle. The blast sent an avalanche of rock down the steep face of Iron's Knob swallowing the coyote in stones and fire and dust.

"Nick!" Coyote Man yelled.

"What's happened to you, Ramani?" Cyril asked, giving Sindra a nudge to keep her moving.

Coyote Man ambled toward Nick. "We got to see if he's still kicking."

Cyril moved to intercept Coyote Man, sliding in front of him with both his hands on Coyote Man's chest. "We're not derailing our escape for some cur."

"That cur saved my life." He pulled up both arms and

spread them between Cyril's hands, throwing Cyril into a seated position on the boulder behind them.

"Figures. Curs stick together." Cyril rose to his feet. "Shoulda let you die with dignity—instead of turning you into some savage."

Nick had a piece of his ear missing. He was covered in splotches of mangy fur, and he fed on what rotted that the sandy wind hadn't yet whittled to bone dust. But Nick possessed more dignity in his tail alone than Cyril ever had. "Who's the savage?"

Cyril snapped his fingers. "Changed my mind. I am going to see about that animal, and if that blast didn't kill that fool cur then I'll do it." He pointed a finger at the middle at his forehead and lifted his thumb as if shooting a pistol.

"Not if I croak you first."

The steel in Coyote Man's eyes frightened Sindra. She backed away, jerking free of Cyril's grasp as Coyote Man wrapped his hands around Cyril's throat. Cyril hacked and threw his arms up to block him. His eyes bulged, and his face turned a shade of pink before transforming to bright red. With his right arm, Cyril groped the ground for his pistol. Sindra saw the barrel of the gun sticking into Coyote Man's gut with Cyril's finger searching for the trigger.

Without thinking, Sindra rammed Cyril off balance. They all fell into a rocky depression with Cyril still gasping for air as Coyote Man struggled to regain his grip on his countryman's throat. Without the use of her hands, Sindra wormed her way to her feet. The two men rolled away from her, and as Coyote Man rolled on top, Sindra kicked Cyril in the the ribs.

A muffled clap sounded from the fray. Coyote Man's

grip loosened. Cyril stood up with the gun still in his hand and shoved Coyote Man back. His limp body rolled down the slope into a dark ravine. "There. He and *Nick* can find the Great Above together."

Cyril turned to Sindra and punched her in the face. She twisted around, smacking the ground without her hands to break her fall. "Kick me again and you'll join them. I don't like killing. But I've done what I've had to do to win this war." He jerked her to her feet and pushed her forward. "Look at it this way. I'll be a hero. And that means you'll be a hero's wife."

"You'll have to kill me first."

"Live trophy or a dead hill monkey."

They reached the summit of Iron's Knob with only remnants of daylight remaining. From here, Sindra could see the Jonesbridge defense artillery returning fire through a curtain of black smoke in a fierce battle for the Jones' Bridge, the only bridge that spanned the Great Gorge. The Gorge had not been wide enough to thwart the long range shells as was once believed, but it was far enough for the shells to fall short of the factories when the enemy finally arrived, just as Myron had predicted they would.

Cyril kept his eyes focused on the bridge gate, as if he expected an Eastern Bloc battalion to march right through, flag unfurled to finally claim their prize and adorn Cyril with a medal on the spot.

"You know," he said, gazing at the bridge, "five years ago, when I first realized we finally had *visual confirmation* of this place, me and Ramani stood almost in this very spot. We underestimated you. I had never seen so much industry. This is really it. The heart of what keeps you kicking, year after year, drawing out a war you'll never win."

Leaning against an embankment, almost lying down, Sindra shivered as the air grew colder. The wind on Iron's Knob howled across the Gorge, carrying clouds of spent ordinance. "I don't care about this stupid war or your worthless victories." Sindra coughed. "Just let me go. I'll never be your trophy anyway."

"Shut up. I'll talk. You listen." When Sindra saw Cyril's foot cock, readying to kick her, she twisted around to let her ribs take the blunt of the blow, protecting her abdomen and her unborn child at all costs, now confident she'd thrown up the black whisper concoction before it had worked its dark magic.

Cyril tethered Sindra to a shin pine branch next to an outcropping, and for two hours while Cyril stared at the bridge, she managed some wiggle room in the cords around her wrists. When she felt the strips loosen, she squirmed for relief, but her movement didn't go unnoticed.

"Don't get any crazy notions about running off." Cyril kept one eye on the bridge as he ripped more burlaps strips. He patted along the contours of Sindra's legs stopping for a grab of flesh mid-thigh before making his way to her feet, tying them together in another knot so tight, Sindra feared she would lose feeling below her ankles. With hope for any chance for escape dwindling, she tried to come up with another plan. "Not so tight. If I'm going to be your trophy, you'll want to take care with me, right?"

"Even weathered and damaged a bit, you'll make a fine prize next to what passes for a woman around here." Cyril loosened the strap around her ankles a little, but added an extra tie around her knees. With one hand still between her legs, he groped his way up her waist. Sindra bit down, thrusting her knees up against Cyril's chest.

"Won't be long now," he said, staring at the bridge gate.

Lying on the ground, Sindra watched the puffs of smoke from artillery fire drift across the sky like little balls of brown cotton. She concentrated on fonder times, like rail-walker stories around the campfire and about the airship that Myron had crafted from scraps that he promised would sail them over the Gorge. Feet leaving the ground, head floating above the smoke, it was a sensation she got just thinking about Myron, taking flight with some of his hope.

"Sure is taking them a while," Sindra said with a hoarse voice that took more energy to produce than she had expected.

"They'll be here. No way those scrawny defenses can hold us off much longer. I just hope they don't get desperate and try to destroy that bridge or we'll all be stuck here."

"You may have more firepower, but I'll bet we're smarter."

"Shut your mouth." Cyril stood up and smacked her across the face with the butt of his pistol.

The pain jolted her all the way to the roots of her teeth. Sindra struggled as he gagged her, fought with her tongue, trying to spit the gag out, biting down hard on the fabric the way she wished she had bitten down on those ghosts every time they had tried to force themselves on her.

"My old man kept a wench like you. Healthy and nice to look at. And feisty, just like you. Avalina. A carpie that worked the shack by the River Hudson. Old man took me down there when I turned twelve to let her turn me into a man." Cyril never took his eyes off the gate. "I did make my manhood that day, but not before she gave me a good kick in the bull eggs for her trouble."

Sindra squirmed, tried to protest through the gag, but her whole body ached, fatigued to the point of paralysis. Her lips were parched and her stomach groaned, and she was not going to be caged again, so while the Jonesbridge gate held Cyril in a trance, she kept patient, enduring his yammering until she could work free, even if it took the time for the moon to wend across the sky before it settled in the haze behind Patriot's Pass.

As discretely as she could, she maneuvered Sindra's Star out of her smock hem, having earlier in the day cursed its sharp points as she heaved Myron's litter around boulders the size of overloaders. Her wrists stung every time she worked her fingers along the burlap, the same sensation that had begun to burn her face where the gag tugged at her cheeks.

Cyril finally looked down at Sindra. She immediately stopped sawing, lying as still as she could. "It's a shame you're tainted. Hips like that, you might have been able to have a strong baby. You'll make a fine carpie wife, though."

"I am *not* a carpie." She considered her life the past few months. "Not by choice." The tone in Cyril's voice when he said the word *baby* reminded her of how valuable new, healthy life in this wasteland really was. "And I'm not tainted, either. I, I'm pregnant right now."

"You're lying." Cyril rolled Sindra on her back and lifted her smock. Her whole body clenched when his hand touched her abdomen. "Look at that." His hand followed the slight outward contour from her belly button to the tops of her thighs. Sindra squirmed away. "Hell, I'm going home a hero *and* a father." He stepped away gazing back at the bridge again and returned with a blanket that he spread out over her.

Sindra's hands and feet had been in so much pain that she had almost forgotten the misery of lying on the frozen ground until the warmth of the blanket brought feeling back to her extremities. As soon as Cyril looked away, she began to hack through the burlap again, popping the thin strands one at a time with the star instead of trying to muscle through a thick clump of rope. Under the cover of a blanket, she finally had an opportunity to work free. The strap grew thinner with every minute, and as she pulled hard, finally a warm relief spread across her hands as the grip loosened, thankful again for the little star in her pocket that guided her way.

Flashes from artillery shells lit the horizon again. Loud booms from inside the Gorge rumbled beneath them. Cyril stood up, hands on his hips, gazing into the smoky horizon at the bridge. She wondered what he expected—a throng of merrymakers dancing across the bridge to whisk the hero and his trophy off to a delightful victory feast? She imagined that living in Jonesbridge all these years, pretending to be a patriotic administrator, thoughts of this day had eaten holes in his thinking the way a moth consumed cloth.

Sindra wiggled her legs and knees free with her feet soon to follow. She rested for a few minutes, gathering her strength, knowing she had one good shot at making her escape. She scanned the ground in the campfire's light, in search of a fist-sized stone within her reach, and mentally calculated the distance. Then she loosened her gag.

"Cyril," she whispered. "I know I don't matter, but think of the baby." She readied herself, legs in position under the blanket. "It's so cold. Two people are warmer than one."

Saying those words made her feel sick.

He ambled toward her, looking over his shoulder in the direction of the gate. "Shh. You hear that? *Quiet.* The bombs have stopped." He reached down to put the the gag back in her mouth and settle under the blanket with Sindra as she suggested.

When his fingers came near, she bit down with all the power of her jaw.

Cyril yelled. Sindra hopped to her feet, the numbness in her legs from hours in one position made her wobble, almost sending her back to the ground.

When Cyril got to his feet, Sindra kicked him right in the bull eggs. While he was doubled over, she raced for the rock she had spotted and gave the back of his head a smack. Cyril's body flattened out on the ground. Sindra eyed the spot of blood on his head and rolled him over with her foot, shoving him again until he tumbled down the hill into darkness.

Glistening in the firelight, Sindra spotted Cyril's gun. She picked it up, and closing one eye, she peered down the barrel then turned it around so that the handle fit in her hand. Fearful of the power it possessed, she threw it down and gathered as much of Cyril's gear as she could carry before racing toward the bunker, praying Myron was still alive.

CHAPTER 17

Out of breath from her escape, Sindra heaved the door of the bunker open to find Myron splayed out on a bench beneath the turret. His color didn't look right, like the snow in Jonesbridge, a bit gray, yellow around the eyes. He was still breathing. She could see his chest rising and falling, but he looked as though he had already died. "Wake up, Lalana. Myron looks awful," she yelled, rushing down the steps.

Lalana and Errol were asleep, huddled up together at the foot of the steep concrete stairway of the bunker. Lalana's eyes popped open. Disoriented, she cast a bleary eye at Myron and clicked her tongue. "Lordy. He does look bad. I'm afraid that slug has to come out."

"Can you do it?"

"I was hoping it wouldn't come to that." Lalana cocked her head and put a hand on Errol's shoulder, hoisting herself to her feet. "First, I'll need to whip up a batch of blister back." She took inventory of her bag, mumbling, pulling out jars and cinched bags. "Garlic concentrate. Bit of silver. Horn bind. Infection's a worry. Specs too small to see can kill a man as sure as any piss whistle." Even as cold as it was, Sindra noticed a bead of sweat on Lalana's brow. "Going to need something sharper than a charred stick to finagle that bullet out, though."

Sindra fiddled with the star in her pocket that had already saved her life once today and held it out for Lalana. Sindra ran her finger over the scrawled letters. *Sindra's star.* It made her want to learn how to read words, recognize her name, and spot the shape of the letters that formed words like *star*.

"Where did you get that?" It was jagged in places, but at least one side had been hammered to a smooth point. Lalana handed Errol a flint rock to get a hot fire going outside to sterilize the blade. She pulled Myron's good leg out of the way. Kneeling down beside his wound, she unwrapped the burlap knots around his leg. "Uh oh."

"What is it?"

"Looks like he's coming around. I sure hoped he'd be out cold for this part."

Sindra studied each line in Myron's face, his nose, the length of his eye lashes. He was certainly handsome in his way, with jaws and cheeks as though they were hewn from sandstone. His eyes were as big as his dreams, and seeing them open again renewed her faith that they could somehow make it out of here.

Myron coughed and mumbled then he tried to sit up. He fell back down with a moan. "We have to go."

"This'll pain you up something awful." Lalana shoved some dried leaves into his mouth. "Under the tongue. That's all the billet thistle I got left."

"How you doing with that star?"

"Here it is. Nice and hot."

"No." Myron struggled to sit up until Sindra held him down. "Don't burn any of that coal." Myron blurted out his protest with a shallow breath. "It'll take every bit of it to get us over the Gorge."

Lalana pulled out a short length of rope from her bag. "I'm cutting into you now, Myron. Bite down on this rope."

"What happ—" Myron stopped mid-sentence when Lalana spread the wound open. He bit down on the rope, his face pulling in opposite directions as though he had a hook in each side of his mouth.

"Keep him still," Lalana said.

"I'm trying!" Myron's shoulders tensed, the tendons in his neck drew taut.

"There you are," Lalana whispered as she fished for the bullet. "Trying to hide from me, but I see you."

Sindra's eyes passed between the agony on Myron's face, all the blood seeping onto the bench, and the concentration on Lalana's face as she navigated Myron's wound, taking care not to rip flesh with the other points of the star.

Lalana smiled and dropped a blood-streaked metal fragment into Sindra's hand. "Errol, stoke your fire."

Sindra held her hand behind Myron's head when the air filled with the odor of burning flesh as Lalana cauterized the wound.

"Is he going to make it?" Sindra whispered.

"He's got as good a chance as any of us, now. Lordy knows what's going to roll across that bridge," Lalana said. She tied two fresh burlap strips around Myron's leg and leaned back with a sigh. "Time to rest, now. Everybody needs a bit of sleep."

Lalana put them at ease telling stories of her childhood and her life of working on the last menagerie train with her father. After that, they fell asleep to the sounds of her voice, humming a mournful tune.

Myron had a fitful sleep. His wound throbbed and itched as he dreamed of giant beasts feasting on his leg, like those in the traveling menagerie Lalana described after the surgery, with stripes and horns and long necks. He'd slept in Sindra's arms, and every time he awoke to what he thought were the sounds of the factory floor, Sindra's hand patted his chest back to sleep.

He wanted to wake up, but he couldn't open his eyes, as he tried to emerge from a deep hole, taking hollow breaths, drowning in black nothingness instead of water. Finally he pried his eyes open, expecting to feel comforted, finally with Sindra. Instead, he awoke confused and disoriented, first, in a field behind his grandfather's house, then, seeing the empty room, back in his quarters in 14-C. He rubbed his eyes and sat up. The pain in his leg jarred his memory.

When he lifted his head, the world spun. He looked around, concrete walls, narrow strip of daylight. After a few moments, in the violet of dawn filtering through the turret vent, his environment came into focus. The bunker, he remembered. "We made it."

After all the planning and work, the time had come. They were here. They had the pieces. He could assemble the airship, and they could make their flight over the Gorge. But problems he hadn't anticipated quashed Myron's excitement. When he planned his original escape, he'd counted on having a blanket of smoke from the factories to hide in as he crossed the Gorge. And on a sunny day, with the threat of E'ster artillery, his airship would resemble a swollen tick hanging in the sky waiting to be popped. If they waited until nighttime—the E'sters would probably have taken Jonesbridge by then. Compounding the danger, there were now more people. He and Sindra, they might be able to make it, but Errol, he'd want to escape, too, and Lalana, and Coyote Man. That would be far too much weight to make it.

Considering the possibilities, Myron grew nauseous. E'ster artillery—it was either that or contend with the Jonesbridge watchtowers, so he checked that one off in his mind as a wash. The clear sky versus nighttime—he didn't see waiting as an option. The extra weight, though—he did have an idea for how he could solve that dilemma.

The situation resembled the word problems in his ancient physics book. Even loaded with all the extra weight, if it flew at all, his balloon full of hot air wouldn't fall right out of the sky. It would descend. How rapidly, he didn't know. He could think of only one accessible hill tall enough, with enough clearance: the summit of Iron's Knob. And at the bunker, they were already halfway to the top.

"We don't have much time. We have to assemble the airship and get it to the top of Iron's Knob." He stopped to catch his breath, surprised at how exhausted he was. "That's the only way we'll all make it across."

"Oh Lordy. That's crazy talk. That mess of a contraption out there is a death trap."

Errol lifted up off the bench and leaned on the wall. "You're a good kid, a survivor. We're all survivors. That's why we're here and not dead in a heap." He pointed to the embattled hillside. "I want out of this place, same as you.

But if I wanted to off myself, I can think of fifty ways I'd rather go than falling out of the sky. Rethink this craziness," he nodded at Sindra, "for her sake."

Myron tried to stand and fell against the wall. Pain radiated from his wound all the way to his chest. His blood rushed to his head, and the four concrete walls spun. Rays of daylight scattered through the turret vent. He stabilized himself against the wall and stumbled for the stairs, not looking at Sindra, afraid to see hesitation on her face, too. He conceded that the airship didn't look like much in its current state, but if he assembled it, they would see, they would understand that it could work. "Coyote Man, he thinks it'll work."

"That wild man is dead. He was an E'ster spy, anyway, he and that administrator fellow," Lalana said.

"But Coyote Man changed," Sindra insisted. "I saw him. He wasn't really an E'ster. Not anymore."

As peculiar as Coyote Man was, this news struck Myron. He'd grown to like him. His survival out on the rim had inspired Myron, and in some ways, maybe it was his beard, he reminded him of his grandfather.

Sindra threw Myron's arm over her shoulders and helped him up the stairs. Limping out of the bunker, Myron gazed up to where they would have to begin their decent, to the hill's crest that cast a jagged shadow across the creek bed.

Lalana used her hand as a visor, shielding the glare from the sun as she gazed into the valley. "The stables. That's really the best place to hide out, for now, anyway. We won't starve if we go there. Plus there ain't nothing there the E'sters want."

Errol searched the ground for a suitable walking stick.

"Think this through."

"Come with us," Lalana said. "I have more medicines for that wound down there, too."

Myron finally mustered the courage to look at Sindra, unsure of what he would do or say if he spotted doubt in her eyes, how he would convince her, but she looked back at him, her resolve unmoved, and took his hand. "We're going over the Gorge. And we're not stopping until we run out of coal."

Lalana clicked her tongue. "If you young ones are the future, I'm sorry to say I don't think we have one. This may very well be the end." She motioned Errol to begin their journey back.

Myron and Sindra exchanged glances, as though one or the other would call out to stop Errol and Lalana from leaving, but neither spoke as they watched them amble down the creek bed in the direction of Old Town.

"We *are* going to make it, Myron."

"One step closer to Bora Bora."

Myron instinctively searched the fold in his smock until he remembered that they'd taken everything when he was arrested. His postcard of Bora Bora had moored him to his dream, and having it confiscated by the ghosts, no longer able it to look at to reassure him, to infuse his plan with hope, left him as rudderless as the day he first received it.

• • •

Myron followed his grandfather to the barn, turning his head away as he did every time he passed the set of two graves, his mother's flanked by his own that had kept him out of the hands of the orange shirts for ten years. When the barn door creaked open, his grandfather pulled a canvas tarp from a pile in the corner, the only part of the barn that had been off limits since Myron's mother died. Myron spotted the large basket stuffed with a giant roll of fabric.

"Why now?"

"My gut says go now." His grandfather tugged the basket into the open field. "The older you get, the more you trust your gut over your heart."

"Where can we go?" Myron had always believed that nothing remained of what he'd read about in the books, envisioning only wasteland beyond Richterville.

Myron's grandfather reached into the chest beside the basket and pulled out a worn rectangle of cardboard. He handed it to Myron with a rare smile. "Maybe here."

The colors on the card struck Myron, green and blue, a bright yellow sun overhead and waves lapping at a sandy shore, two arching palm trees and a bird soaring out to sea. Two words written at an angle across the top read *Bora Bora* in faded letters.

Beside his mother's keepsakes, Myron spotted two Old Age books, *The Atlas of the Modern World*, and a physics book, along with a few other odds and ends, such as a fishing lure and bob. "Almost ready."

Myron ambled over to a large metal pan where his grandfather stoked coal. Above the pan, the lightweight cloth billowed from a folded apron into a wavering patchwork cloud of hundreds of beige and blue and orange swatches sewn together in irregular patterns. "This, my boy, is not *just* a balloon," his grandfather said, holding his hand out over the seat. "*This* is an airship." He yanked two levers up and down as a triangle-shaped rudder creaked back and forth over the propeller. "A balloon goes where the wind takes it. An airship goes where the pilot takes it."

Myron settled into the basket next to his grandfather. The bellows stoked the coal. The airship swayed, lifted off the ground, and drifted over the barn, over the two family graves. Behind him, the tiny house Myron had lived in the last eleven years shrank into the background.

"Look down there," his grandfather pointed to a row of black chimneys, each one with a trail of gray searching for an air current. They looked so strange from above, like hundreds of little mouths blowing out pipe smoke. The air was thick with brown and gray until, at last, they rose high enough to breech the low hanging smoke clouds.

Myron was afraid to speak, as though a sky that clear might shatter like a pane of window glass. The harder Myron pedaled, working the bellows, turning the propeller, the hotter the fire in the bin, and they continued to rise.

Up to that moment, that was the greatest day of Myron's life. His grandfather placed a hand firmly on Myron's knee, a worried look in his eyes. The airship wobbled, and the coal pan creaked. "What's going on?"

"I don't know. Too much weight, maybe."

The basket under them moaned, followed by a snapping noise above them. One by one, white-hot coals slipped out of the bottom of the broken coal pan, streaking sparks and ash across the sky. "The coal!" Myron and his grandfather squirmed to avoid getting burned. The supply chest came loose.

Myron reached for the handle on the chest. The ground spun in the hazy distance beneath them. "I got it." Leaning over the side, holding the chest by one arm, the airship tilted, spilling more of the coal.

"We're going down." The balloon billowed above them and they began to descend. "Drop the chest, Myron. Hurry!"

"I can't."

"You have to. Now."

Myron yanked the chest up and flung the lid open. With his free hand he snagged the postcard of Bora Bora and anything else he could grasp. "We need something to stabilize the coal pan."

Below them, on the main road, a whole squad of orange shirts had assembled, pointing to the deflating balloon, trying to pinpoint the spot the airship would land.

Myron's grandfather spoke quickly as the ground continued to rise. "Listen well. If you get away, if you want to survive, make them think you are as dumb as a post and ready to serve." He whispered faster as a group of orange-shirts assembled directly beneath them. "When I give the signal, run. Just like you did that day, but, this time don't come back. Run, walk, fly, swim as far as you can go."

"What about you?"

The men in orange gathered around the collapsing balloon as Myron and his grandfather made a hard landing. Myron tucked the postcard of Bora Bora and anything else he'd rescued from the chest into his jacket.

"How old are you?" The leader of the orange shirts stood over Myron.

"Seventeen." Myron stood up, looking to his grandfather for a signal.

"*Seventeen?* This kid's been shirking out here for ten years." He scowled at Myron. "Name?"

"Myron Daw."

"Okay. Ship *Myron* here off to Jonesbridge."

They reached for Myron's arm, and his grandfather gave him the signal. "Dispose of the old man."

Hearing those words, Myron counted the orange shirts, calculated the odds of winning a fight and broke for the hillside, running until his legs felt like melted butter ahead of the footsteps of cursing orange-shirts. When he reached the draw on the other side of the hill, confident he'd escaped, Myron stopped to catch his breath and look behind him for the first time.

"Gotcha."

He caught only a glimpse of orange before a burlap sack slipped over his head and cinched up around his neck.

• • •

Myron clutched his leg and eased down beside the airship basket. He unpacked a bundle near the balloon, and a variety of nuts and bolts spilled out onto the ground. Sorting through them, finding the largest of the group, he attached the propeller to the pedal gear behind the basket.

As he viewed the pile of junk in front of him, not the grand design he envisioned while he relayed materials the past few months, he understood Errol and Lalana's reservations and plunged into doubt himself. The base structure looked solid, though: a basket he'd woven from pine bark, roots, and burlap by twining them around six of the longest, rigid shin-pine trunks he had found. Incorporating the same technique for the propeller blades and rudder made the whole thing look like furniture someone might find on an island like Bora Bora. The only metal on the contraption was the pedals to turn the propeller, salvaged off a bicycle carcass near the chapel.

Myron's hands trembled as he filled the pots with the hot coals, white sides up, now thankful that Errol had gotten the fire started. He assembled the bellows for stoking the fire and fitted the nozzle into a hole at the base of the coal pot before making his final adjustments. He limped backward to admire his creation. His stomach fluttered, picturing the view of the Gorge from above. The soiled, grayish fabric began to expand as he stoked the coals.

With the airship assembled, Myron searched the ground for the stabilizer, something that might have saved them the day his grandfather's airship went down. It was a long piece of wood with fasteners at each end to keep the basket from moving around too much as the coal burned and shifted. "One more piece. I can't find it."

He tied the airship down as it had already begun to lift. Pain shot through his leg as he limped toward the bunker to comb the entire area where they'd all helped move the airship parts. A light snow began to fall, powdery and brown before it ever hit the ground, but they still had a clear view of the valley. Myron and Sindra held hands without looking at one another, fixated on a squad of ghosts headed their way, double time, gesturing at the enormous mass of ladies' sanitaries, now a balloon, billowing on the hillside.

CHAPTER 18

Sindra scanned the ground for the missing airship piece, but the rising balloon, made of discarded underwear, stole her attention.

"What does it look like?" Sindra combed the area around the bunker.

"Long and thin. It's not here." Myron ducked into the bunker. "It's a stabilizer." The concrete muffled his voice.

Sindra gazed into the valley and saw that the orange shirts had made it halfway up the hill. "Do we have to have it?"

"I don't know." Myron emerged from the bunker, his face pale.

"What do you mean, you don't know?" Sindra heard the crunching of boots on snow. "Come on, Myron." She tugged at his smock.

"Last time, with my grandfather, we almost crashed without it."

"Shh." She pointed to the other side of the draw.

Myron kept his eyes on the ground, studying every rock and twig in search of his stabilizer. Sindra yanked him by the smock. When he refused to give up the search and make a run for the airship, Sindra grabbed him by the hair and pulled him toward her, gritting her teeth and nodding toward the balloon that sat against the sky like a boil in need of lancing. Given their two options, crashing into the Gorge or letting the ghosts get them, she chose the Gorge.

Myron hobbled toward the airship in a daze, dragging the foot of his injured leg. Sindra threw his arm over her shoulder as they ran together, certain she could smell the breath of the ghosts panting behind them. Jonesbridge would not get them again, even if she had to drag Myron by his toes and toss him into the basket herself.

As they rounded the creek bed, Sindra cringed to see Coyote Man standing inside the airship basket stoking the coals.

"You weren't thinking of leaving without *me*, were you?" Coyote Man said. A streak of dried blood ran from the side of his head down his neck. He was covered in red dust, and all that remained of his coyote skins dangled from his shoulders in shreds. "Come on. Let's get out of here." Coyote Man waved them on.

"Don't move. The rope has come untied." Myron pointed at the rope dragging the ground while the unmoored balloon drifted toward the cliff on a strong wind.

"Wait," Sindra yelled. Coyote Man had showed up yet again to stick his dirty foot in the middle of the stew pot. She'd watched Cyril shoot him and roll him down the hill, and here he was, standing in the airship basket drifting away without them. No, not this time; he wouldn't scare them away or make them change their plans, or whack one of them over the head or sabotage their escape, not again. Sindra dropped Myron and sprinted full speed for the airship to get enough of the rope to tie it back down.

"How do you stop this thing?" Coyote Man leaned over the edge of the basket as it rose.

Sindra leaped from rock to rock, reaching for the rope that slipped through her hands before she got a grip on it.

"Sindra. Wait," Myron called.

Wait? If they waited, they'd be stuck here forever. Their future now floated away without them. Waiting was over. She had to act fast so that her child, if she still carried one, and she was confident she did, would be born somewhere other than Jonesbridge, so that Myron could be the father, and after that, the rest of the world could wash down into the Chasm for all she cared. Sindra jumped again for the rope, this time getting a solid grip with both hands. "I've got it, Myron." The basket drifted back down until Sindra's feet slid across the rocks, skidding like a sled.

"Sindra let go," Myron hollered.

She heard Myron but couldn't believe her ears. He wanted her to just let go and leave their entire lives to the whims of the orange shirts over the next ridge.

"Sindra!"

She tightened her grip and widened her stance, digging the knife-edge of her foot into the ground, but the balloon lifted her just enough to keep her from getting traction. Determined to save the airship, Sindra wrapped the rope around her hands and gripped as tight as she could. Her feet skipped over the ground as she yanked down. With all of her concentration on the rope and tuning out Myron's calls for her to stop, her stomach leaped when the ground beneath her gave way to empty space. The airship slipped over the edge of the cliff with her hanging beneath it, a hundred feet above a ravine. The balloon dipped, and Sindra swung until it stabilized in an upward tack.

"Go back!" Sindra clung to the rope. The bottom of the airship basket spun above her.

"Rudder's not working," Coyote Man shouted.

"Peddle."

"Myron!"

"Hang on, Sindra. Don't look down."

With each twirl around on the rope, Sindra watched Myron grow smaller against the hillside. The horizon expanded into a gaping mouth of landscape, mountains, crags, clouds, against a field of snow pellets, and the sharp points of the earth beneath her made her stomach drop. The gray from Myron's smock blended with the rocks on Iron's Knob until he vanished, but she could still see his face in her mind, his wet eyes, the furrows in his cheeks as he stretched to reach her.

"Bora Bora," Myron whispered.

He fell back against the hillside and watched the airship dodge in and out of a cloud bank until it diminished from a blotch to a spot and finally to a spec, with Sindra still on the rope. The pain in his leg screamed. Myron grabbed his thigh and punched his wound. He winced and doubled over before punching it again. If he hadn't gotten injured, none of this would have happened. He would have been there with Sindra, standing beside her in that basket reaching for the sky together. He punched his leg again, and his eyes welled with tears as he rolled on the ground moaning. If he'd ignored the pain and chased her, ran as fast as he could, their weight together would have held it down. He punched again and screamed. His leg pinked under the bandage. Tears he could never muster in the dry wind of Jonesbridge flowed from his eyes. Myron found something in Sindra, more freedom than Bora Bora, more liberation than escape, true feelings for another person, and now she was gone.

He heard voices over the ridge. Ghosts advanced, and in the distance E'ster artillery still rumbled through the hills. He pulled himself forward by his hands, legs sliding behind him like a rock lizard that had lost its tail from fright. The mill pond, his grandfather's library, afternoons in the barn; Myron summoned as many happy memories as he could to supplant the pain in his leg and the loss of Sindra, but all he could see was her face. He struggled to the top of the hill to hide in the shadow of the peak, his eyes still wet from tears and the sting of snow pellets.

From the summit of Iron's Knob, Myron could identify the Yarin Canal, the devastated Munitions factory, Machine and Die, the salvage factory, and the row upon row of chimney stacks for the smelters and refineries that followed the Yarin from the aqueduct all the way to the Gorge. Beyond that, the maw of the salvage pit, where every war-twisted piece of wreckage began its new life, stretched for nearly a mile along the back side of the complex.

That's where he had to go, the salvage pit. He could find all sorts of material there to build another airship. Coal, where would he find more coal? And fabric? If not an airship, maybe a pair of gliding wings or a pedal copter. With the right wind he could glide across the Gorge and catch up with Sindra, and everything could still be fine. He could help her raise the baby. They could still make it to Bora Bora. He could do it. Salvage was what he was good at, and that's what he had to do. Salvage parts. Salvage the situation. Salvage this disaster.

When Myron first arrived in Jonesbridge, when they'd assigned him to salvage, it had been the pit where he began his service. All day in all weathers, cataloguing, sorting, hauling, rummaging through endless stacks of intertwined junk. Myron had identified with the rubbish in the pit, abused, relocated, changed, and as Jonesbridge tried to recycle him into a new thing, the way it did everything else, he had resisted. He'd never heard of a slog until he got to Jonesbridge, but that's what they called him. He ate what slogs ate, worked where slogs worked, and lived like a slog. He didn't know if he was a slog or not, but one thing he knew for certain, he was a natural salvager just like his grandfather.

The salvage pit was the largest work area in all of Jonesbridge, and for this reason it stood outside the confines of the fence. It was bound on the west by the Gorge, on the east by the train depots where the mangled rubbish arrived. The incinerator complex hemmed it in on the south, and on the north end, an over-mined quarry abandoned decades ago.

Myron trudged down the steep side of the hill. His leg ached with every step as he crossed the valley on the shadow side of Iron's Knob where the promontory loomed over him. He froze at the quarry's edge when he heard voices.

Two men emerged at the top of the narrow road that spiraled down into the excavation. Myron dropped to all fours and wiped his eyes. Though he had never seen him in person, the man in front Myron recognized immediately from his posters, the Superintendent of Industry. He sported a thick mustache that twisted up at the ends, grayer than in his pictures, and a full head of hair, also streaked with gray. He resembled the people in Myron's books from the Old Age: strong, able, determined. Behind him, Cyril followed with a gun to the Superintendent's head. After all that Cyril had done to try to get out of Jonesbridge and join his fellow E'sters, Myron questioned why he was here, kidnapping the Superintendent himself, if not to find another way out.

Myron followed at a safe distance into the quarry until the two men disappeared into an opening near the bottom. One explosion after another rumbled in the nearby Gorge, artillery shells and bombs falling short of Jonesbridge. A couple of explosions vibrated the ground as Myron followed the overgrown quarry road until he reached the shelter of an entrance in the stone where he found a heavy metal door standing ajar.

Myron reached for the door and hesitated. He was accustomed to hiding from the orange shirts, avoiding the administrators, keeping low and out of sight, the only way he could have built his airship and stayed alive. Following the most powerful man in Jonesbridge and an E'ster spy into a mysterious door at the bottom of a quarry cut across the grain of his instincts, but if there was even a chance of another way out of Jonesbridge, of another way of reaching Sindra, he could set aside his fear in exchange for hope.

The door creaked open to an empty concrete room no larger than the stretcher chamber. To his right, a concrete shaft plummeted into darkness, closed off by a gate, and flanked by a little red button that tempted Myron to press it. When he did, machinery groaned below the floor. Steam blasted from a vent, and the floor in the smaller chamber rose from the darkness to reveal an elevator.

He stepped in under a bundle of severed wires that dangled from the ceiling and took a deep breath before pulling the lever to his left. When the gate closed, darkness and fear enveloped him the way it had when his grandfather shut the door on the potato bin with the orange shirts right outside.

The machinery rumbled, and the descent made his stomach twitch. A wall of stone zipped passed him on the other side of the gate. He stood in the center with his legs spread apart, expecting to fall into the Chasm itself, until the elevator slowed to a stop and jolted up before inching downward to a stop. Myron faced a concrete corridor illuminated by dim bulbs and a breath of stagnant air that smelled like a musty dead yard.

A sign covered in dust hung in an alcove beside the elevator. Myron wiped it clean with his smock.

Stony Mountain Facility - R1

Below it, a black circle with three yellow triangles read:

Fallout Shelter.

Two explosions rocked the ground above him. Dust and pebbles rained down from cracks in the ceiling. Ahead in the corridor, a chunk of concrete rattled loose and tumbled onto the floor. Myron braced against the wall. Another percussive blast opened a hairline crack in the ceiling. A moment later, a droplet plopped on Myron's head, followed by another, building into a rivulet that trickled to the corner and down the wall.

He ventured down the corridor until he spotted a control room with a large window housing a broken pane of glass three inches thick. He straddled the sill and entered a room that contained two desks with matching chairs and a skeleton slumping in the corner that stared at him with black sockets. A bank of dead computers with black screens ran along the wall. He gazed at their keyboards filled with squares, each one bearing a letter.

He stepped over an empty box on the floor bearing the same curious red symbol he'd seen on the ration crates and on a lot of the materials in the salvage line, but this box also had a word with the symbol: *biohazard*. Myron's stomach wrenched to think that the symbol on their food crates meant biohazard. What sort of hazard? Had it been grown in tainted ground? Made from toxic ingredients? Spoiled ingredients?

He inspected the room and found a desk. From one of the drawers, he found a binder that he opened up on the desk. The cover read:

- *U.S. Air Force.*
- *Stony Mountain Facility.*
- *Standard Operating Procedures for Containment Protocols.*

Inside he spotted signed revisions of procedures from 1973, 1977, 1979, 1983, 1987, and nothing again until 2037, nearly two hundred years ago.

Myron ran his finger down the table of contents, encountering complex words and ideas he wasn't sure about, but he froze when he reached the last entry: S.L.O.G. Development Lab.

"S-L-O-G," Myron whispered. "Slog?"

Myron stood without moving, his ear tuned to the corridor. He heard no noises, except dripping from cracks in the ceiling, no sign of the Superintendent or the administrator, only the dead eyes of the bones in the corner. Water pooled at his feet. He turned back toward the elevator, torn by his will to find another way out of Jonesbridge and all the possible calamities that he might encounter *if* this corridor wasn't a way under the Gorge but some sort of dead end, a trap ending in a showdown between a lowly slog, the traitor administrator, and the superintendent himself.

As he tiptoed down the corridor, he stopped to listen for movement at every empty door jamb. Every portal that he passed tugged at his curiosity, promising more books and more clues to the past, but he kept his focus on one thing, getting to the other side—until he saw a sign that read: *S.L.O.G.*

As he eased through the opening, unable to resist, the room expanded into a cavernous space surrounded by a catwalk. A giant globe on the left showed a color-coded version of the entire planet with large swaths in red, orange, and smaller zones in green, and a few tiny spots of purple. Beside it, several maps in projection depicted the polar ice caps receding in stages until they finally disappeared. Filling the middle of the room, a laboratory with dark screens and computers ran along the entire perimeter, with one enormous word on each wall. Survival. Longevity. Organic. Genesis.

The ceiling, a semicircular dome, consisted of a close-up map of the purple region. Myron studied it in the dim light and noticed a familiar name right away.

"Richterville." That's where he was from. Of the entire planet, of the thousands of small burgs and cities and regions, they'd singled out Richterville on this map, one of the few towns from the Old Age that actually survived. Myron experienced a burst of hometown pride.

Unsure of what any of it meant, he approached the far wall. Under a screen that filled the upper half of the wall, he saw the words: *Norton Model of Accelerated Adaptation, Richterville Watershed*. Paintings of five men in profile, walking, lined the bottom half of the wall. It reminded him of a progression he'd seen in a science book of the gradual modification of apes into people.

The first image, a fully clothed man, like the people in the Old Age books, stood over a green stalk of wheat. The men grew progressively taller and thinner with less hair, more tinted, thicker skin, and less clothing until the final image showed a naked man with inset eyes, no hair at all, and a body so thin his bones protruded. Like the first, the second man stood over green stalk of wheat but also an orange haystack. The third man stood over a green stalk of wheat, an orange haystack *and* a red biohazard symbol. Myron thought this man looked much like the slogs in Jonesbridge. The fourth stood over only an orange haystack and the red biohazard symbol. The last man in the progression only had the red biohazard symbol next to a star.

He scanned the room for anything he could read, any bits not swallowed and housed in the darkened machines and found only binders labeled "Health and Human Services." The last date he found was 2042, the year before the Zealot War, the year of the flash in the sky that stole the life from all the machines.

"Survival. Longevity. Organic. Genesis." In Jonesbridge they called *him* a slog, the same thing they called the other lowly workers not worthy of warm clothes and rations not marked as biohazards. They gave them abrasive sand to rub off their dirt and just enough water to work up a spit. This room, these depictions, these words from the Old Age, made him think, gave him hope, that maybe there was more to being a slog than just a working class designation.

"This is your last chance to guide me out of here," Cyril shouted from beyond the main corridor wall. Myron jumped, so taken by his discovery that he'd forgotten why he wandered down here in the first place.

Though Myron had never seen the Superintendent until today, he'd heard his voice every day through the speaker box on the factory floor, and in this way, he'd come to fear him the way he would fear an unseen phantom stalking the nighttime. The noises, the voice without a body, he wielded an unknown amount of power, and hearing it in person paralyzed Myron. "I told you. It's blocked. And there's a breach. If we don't get out of here soon, the Gorge is going to swallow this place whole."

CHAPTER 19

Coyote Man peered over the edge of the airship basket to an expanse of jagged countryside, and Sindra screaming at the frayed end of the rope. The slug in his gut radiated sharp pains all the way to his fingers as he reeled her in an inch at a time. With each pull of the rope, the basket tipped, and the disorienting height made him woozy.

"I'm trying," he yelled. "Climb!" He knew how scared Sindra was, but his pain weakened him, so he tuned out her cries for help and concentrated on the rope with slow, steady progress.

"I can't hold on." Sindra yelled. The wind snuffed the rest of her response, but he knew she was cursing him for leaving Myron.

He'd left people behind before, all part of the job, but it had never felt so wrong, never smacked him right in the soft spot in his throat the way separating those two kids had. All he wanted now was to make sure that his mistake wouldn't cost Sindra her life.

The relief that washed over him when Sindra's tuft of blond hair crested the edge of the basket made him forget, for a moment, that he'd never managed to do the right thing. He'd fallen so far from the man he once was, the son of the hero of the Battle of Chesapeake. If he'd been half the man his daddy was, he'd have triumphed on the battlefield and won his very own plot of clean land to farm, maybe found a woman that could stand to look at him for more than one night, but it hadn't turn out that way.

Coyote Man reached for Sindra's arms and hoisted her into the airship. The balloon drooped. The coal pan creaked and sprayed a wisp of ash. Sindra hunched over in the corner of the basket and stared up at up him with big eyes, wet with tears and snow and sweat. She reminded him his own daughter—what she might have looked like if she'd lived to be Sindra's age. He looked away and stoked the coals. A toxic updraft stole his breath when the Great Gorge opened beneath them, and the other side of the divide materialized in the haze.

The landscape reminded him of all he endured to get here, the oppressive heat of summer and the frozen winters, the parched earth tainted with blood and toxins, wandering directionless for months through the Nethers with Cyril who spouted venom for the enemy the entire time, an enemy that turned out to be more humane than his own people.

Sindra hadn't uttered a word since she joined him in the basket. She stared at nothing, frozen mid-sob. He wanted to console her, to apologize for being selfish and stupid, for messing up their escape and breaking the rudder. He longed to hug her and tell her everything would be okay in the end, but as he surveyed the other side of the Gorge, he saw the E'ster camp and realized that everything would not be all right—far from it.

Though he stoked the fire, adding as much coal as would fit, the balloon maintained a gradual descent. "We've got a problem."

Sindra peeked over the edge of the basket. "What?"

"We're going down." He sighed and inspected the balloon. "Or—the ground is higher over there. Can't tell." Either way, their current course would land them in the middle of the E'ster camp.

Sindra moved to the center and peddled, causing the propeller to turn. "So we can't steer, but no way are we going down."

Coyote Man studied the E'ster armaments, giant steam-driven landships constructed from vessels that were no longer sea worthy, rolling on colossal wheels. They were equipped with counterweights and catapults that launched their bombs over the Gorge. They'd edged closer and closer to the Gorge to increase their range until the bows jutted out into the noxious darkness of the abyss. He heard the grind of machinery as the catapults drew taut. The familiar sound made his stomach tighten.

He'd lived as a coyote for three years now. It had saved his life and polished the rust off of his soul, and in that time he'd learned that he had no enemies, no reason to fight anyone for anything other than for his own cave and a sip of water. Now, he had no appetite for returning to the Eastern Bloc, hero or otherwise, or living amongst the humans who'd destroyed everything beautiful in the world.

"I know those people." He pointed to the E'sters.

"The ghosts, yeah, they're bad—but nothing compared to the dregs of humanity the Eastern Bloc sends into battle." He eyed the airship's trajectory. "You'd be better off back there." He gave a nod to Jonesbridge.

"*No*, I wouldn't." Sindra pushed him in the chest.

"Chasm knows what will happen to you down there. I can't protect you from those curs." Crossbow bolts arced up at the airship, the first round falling short. "They've spotted us. Up is the only way. We're too heavy."

Sindra worked the bellows, stoking the fire, blowing onto the coals. "What do we do?"

"This is my fault. I'm the reason they found Jonesbridge in the first place. I'm the reason Myron is back there, and you're up here." He kissed her on the cheek, imagining the kiss he never gave his daughter. "Take care of that baby and ride this thing as far as you can—as *far* as the wind will take you." He thought she could make it. He'd never seen people as resilient and tough as the slogs in Jonesbridge. It seemed that they could endure just about anything that would kill a normal person.

The airship listed when Coyote Man straddled the basket.

"Wait! What are you doing?"

"I'm giving you a chance."

Before finding Jonesbridge, he and Cyril had wandered the Nethers, each of them with a vial of poison on a chain around their necks, an emergency measure in the event that the Nethers swallowed them whole as it had every tracker before them. They could end it all by a stomping on a demon's tail, so they called it, with one bite into the vial.

He'd spent countless hours near death with that vial in his mouth, ready to bite, praying Cyril would crunch down on his first so he could have a moment's peace before doing the same, but Cyril never did. And Jonesbridge would have driven him to use his vial long ago if the orange shirts hadn't taken it when they stripped him clean and left him in the hole for dead, before the coyotes had shown him how a man should live. High over the Gorge, with the wind sweeping his beard, he closed his eyes, picturing a coyote den, and readied himself to finally bite into his vial of poison.

"I'm coming, Nick," he shouted and slid over the edge of the basket.

"No!" Sindra screamed, her eyes trained on Coyote man's fall, arms and legs outstretched until the darkness of the Gorge swallowed him. "I can't do this alone."

As the E'ster landships creaked closer to the rim of the Gorge, maximizing their range, without thinking, Sindra loaded more coal into the pot, and the life inside her gave her abdomen a kick, a tiny confirmation that she truly carried a living being, one that hadn't been snuffed by the black whisper, one who'd survived the shirker coop and starvation, someone she would die to protect.

No time to mourn or cry, no time to regret or give up or feel sorry for herself; she had a responsibility now, a future human growing inside her and a breath of wind to ride on, and no wish to make Coyote man's sacrifice all for nothing. Stoking the coal, refueling, stoking again, heating the fire, white coals, again and again she stoked. "Up. Up, up. Go."

A crossbow bolt penetrated the basket, missing Sindra's leg by a hair. She continued to stoke the fire and noticed that with only her weight, the airship had changed course. The E'ster landships grew smaller beneath her, the E'ster battle cries lost on the wind.

The battlements looked so small and harmless from this height, but the higher she rose, the more formidable the Gorge looked, snaking around Jonesbridge like a tourniquet. The earth groaned, sending a shiver down the length of her body. Behind the line of advancing E'sters, a fissure opened under the weight of the landships as they inched closer to the edge. Their bows creaked and the bank of the Great Gorge gave way beneath the three largest landships, spilling them and their crews into the depths with percussive blasts in succession. A noxious cloud rose from the Gorge followed by more explosions that shot pain through Sindra's ears. A hoard of E'sters ran from the edge, some hanging on to ledges before plummeting with a chunk of earth. A chain of soldiers dangled, hand in hand, until the darkness plucked them from the bank. What was left of the E'ster attack settled back and out of range, but they still numbered in the hundreds.

Sindra kneeled in the basket, afraid to move, as if the higher she ascended the more fragile the sky became, afraid she could shatter it with a single poke. She peeked over the edge, back to Jonesbridge, at the clouds of smoke that suffocated the valley. Somewhere down there she imagined Myron gazing up into the sky, thinking about her. The frigid air gave her chills, and she warmed her hands over the burning coal, adding fresh fuel to the fire.

Alone in the Nethers, a girl, now a woman, pregnant, with no food, no water and no idea which way the wind blew her, except that she sailed toward the setting sun. Not safe to land, not safe to stay up in the air, not safe to set one foot in the dead soil of the Nethers where the carcasses of ancient snakes lay petrified in white chalk, not a safe world for a newborn child nor for her mother, but whatever happened to her now, she would live or die free from the shackles of Jonesbridge.

As she rose above the lower layer of smoke and clouds, the sun, halfway set, fanned rays of pink and orange across the horizon. Sindra marveled at how peaceful and warm the sky over a battlefield could be, a sky marred with the reflection of the dying ground beneath it. When the sun settled behind the blue outline of the mountains, a single star twinkled into view. Sindra patted down her smock in a panic, not feeling its points, praying she hadn't lost it. From the hem of her smock, she pulled out *Sindra's Star* with relief and held it to the horizon with one eye closed, as if to hang it in the sky.

She collected what remained of the coal from the bottom of the basket and put it into the coal bin where the embers popped. The fires of the E'ster battle camp had faded behind her, and the entire heaven of stars opened above her. Nothing but phantom peaks and dark valleys stood between her and the horizon. The silence frightened her. For the first time in her memory, she heard no turbines humming, no groan of machinery, no barges or trains, no whistles or marching feet of workers, only nothingness, as though she had stuffed wads of burlap into her ears.

As much as she wanted to crash the airship and run to the edge of the Gorge to wait for Myron, Coyote Man knew the E'sters, and the Nethers, and he'd given his life for her to ride as far as the wind would take her. Old Nickel used to tell her while walking the rails that trusting feelings over common sense was like leaving a trail of breadcrumbs for the grim reaper to follow, so she would stay airborne as long as she could. Myron was so far away from her now, but she had the star he'd given her and the dreams he'd shown her, and a face to remember, a vision she would keep fresh in her mind to one day describe to the child she carried.

Commited now to her freedom and a new life for her child, Sindra kept the coals hot to get as far away as possible. The higher she rose, the more numbing the air became. Sindra shivered as she stoked the coals, staving off sleep for as long as she could, for what seemed like hours, until she nodded off against the bellows, beside the warmth of the glowing coal.

. . .

Sindra awoke to the sound of water lapping against the airship and a breath of heavy air. A wave sloshed over the side of the basket, adding to the pool of water at her feet. She licked her lips, salt. The water made her skin tingle as she splashed trying to stand up, wrestling with the balloon draped over the coal pan.

Another wave pummeled her across the face as she stared into an endless body of water in front of her, and behind her, dozens of small islands interconnected by salvaged debris. Sindra had heard of great bodies of water, even before she met Myron, but she'd assumed they had either all dried up or were nothing more than Old Age fairy tales. She had always heard the oceans had died, but she'd never wanted to say that to Myron. He'd turned out to be right.

She soaked in the sights of the ocean as she drifted with the current toward the collection of debris, fearful of spike-toothed sea creatures lying in wait for fresh meat. In the side of the largest of the landmasses, tall white letters formed the word, *H—-L-L-Y-W-O—D*. The name of the island or a welcome message, Sindra didn't know, but she wondered if it said Bora Bora, though she had no idea what letters would spell that. If she had found Bora Bora, it looked nothing like Myron's postcard.

Floating bridges constructed of amazing materials like rubber tires, planks on lines of plastic bottles and airplane fuselages, things she'd never seen in the salvage pit, fanned from all sides of the mountain island with the H-llywo-d letters. Salvaged garbage, fashioned into dwellings, covered the entire island except for the area around the letters. Men and women, kids, too, came and went, and along a pier in front of the dwellings, two moored boats bobbed on calm waters, while at the far end of the island, several windmills fashioned from airplane wings churned in the coastal breeze.

When the current brought her to the edge of the pier, Sindra climbed out of the basket, praying she would see no orange shirts or administrators or E'sters with bones in their beards. Her eyes connected with a woman carrying a basket. The woman put the basket down and pointed at Sindra. Several people dressed in patchwork clothes approached, not to arrest her or violate or harm her, but to welcome her. She glanced back in the direction she'd come from, where the haze of the sea had replaced smoke and ash, and knew that if she had made it, thanks to Myron's airship, that Myron could too.

CHAPTER 20

Droplets of water plopping on Myron's head had turned to trickles. The liquid reeked of chemicals, stagnant sludge worse than the Yarin Canal, and Myron was certain that it came from the Gorge, that this R1 Facility from the Old Age spanned the underbelly of the chasm. If the Superintendent had been bluffing when he spoke of a breach, Myron clung to his hope that he could somehow navigate the rubble, something he had gotten good at recently, and emerge on the other side, free from the gravity of Jonesbridge, the way Sindra had.

He edged to the corner and eased his eyes around to see Cyril pointing his pistol at the Superintendent, who stood, as instructed, with his hands locked behind his head.

"Look at it. There's no way through." The Superintendent nodded toward the crumbled corridor, now ankle-deep with water.

As Cyril opened his mouth to reply, an explosion

rocked the ground above them. A concrete beam dislodged, tumbling from the ceiling. It struck Cyril on the head. His body jerked. The gun fired, and the Superintendent fell, face first, into a deepening pool of water.

Myron froze as the ground trembled. He eyed the impassable corridor, scanning for an opening. When he spotted a crawlspace, a gush of water dashed his hopes. After another explosion, he hunkered down, readying himself to make a run back out the way he came, but seeing the Superintendent's arm twitch as he tried to raise himself out of the water made Myron pause.

The ceiling groaned. Cracks opened in the walls. Another explosion. Myron inched toward the Superintendent, keeping an eye out for debris. The Superintendent coughed and hung his head when Myron rolled him over. A trickle of blood seeped from his abdomen. He was unconscious and unresponsive, but he was still alive, while Cyril's run had ended, crushed beneath a pile of concrete.

Myron leaned the Superintendent against a stone block with his head out of the knee-deep water. At its current rate the water would fill the R1 Facility completely with toxic sludge, swallowing Myron, the Superintendent, and all the Old Age evidence of S.L.O.G.'s in less than ten minutes. He could make it if he ran now, but the higher the water rose the harder it would be.

He didn't want to leave the Superintendent, still breathing, to die in the company of the man who'd shot him. But what had the Superintendent done to deserve rescuing? He wore hardy clothing, ate real food, lived in a warm barrack with running water, while Myron rubbed his skin with sand and pissed in the snow. Myron held him responsible for directing the orange shirts to steal the people of Richterville to toil away in Jonesbridge as patriotic slaves, and the one who ordered an execution of the elders, like Myron's grandfather, who either wouldn't have survived the trip, or could no longer work fifteen hour days. A brute, holed up in his tower, who never showed his face to the people he commanded, gracing them with a daily admonition of guilt and fear—*or* was he a hero to the alliance? The one who'd made the tough choices, found workers who could survive the harsh climes of the hills to keep the hope of a people alive. Had he been the one to take charge when all others had lost hope, putting each person to their given duties according to abilities, making use of every resource, evading the E'sters' detection, and saving them all? While Myron fought with his question, the water continued to rise.

He positioned his shoulder on the Superintendent's stomach and hoisted him over his shoulder, slumping under the weight of the man who outweighed him by half. Blood smeared across his arm from the Superintendent's wound. Red hit the water and swirled into a pattern with the black and green slime that floated on top. The lights flickered. Myron trudged through the cavernous map room, allowing the Superintendent's legs to float behind him to alleviate some of the weight.

As the water rose, the air grew noxious. His nose burned. The water stung his skin as though it were filled with prickly pin bushes. The Superintendent groaned. Myron repositioned him and forced through the thigh-high water. Another blast crumbled the wall into the corridor. Water rushed through the ceiling. Myron pulled through the torrent, towing the Superintendent toward the elevator shaft.

As both his legs cramped, he pushed passed the pain, visualizing the images on the S.L.O.G. wall, of the slogs like him and their evolution, who could survive the elements and eat toxic food. Inspired by the thought, he yelled "I am a slog." His voice echoed through the stone corridor until the rising water snuffed it. On the verge of tears, he whispered again with pride, "I am a slog from Richterville." He imagined the super heroes from Old Age story books, transformed by radiation or experimentation that spawned wondrous abilities, making Myron wish being a S.L.O.G meant that he could fly.

At the end of the corridor Myron waded into the elevator. He dropped the Superintendent with a splash and yanked the lever. Steam shot from the vent. It sputtered, and water cascaded from the elevator as it rose and fell trying to escape the weight of the liquid, until enough water spilled from the open elevator door as it rose. Myron slumped in the corner, staring at the bleeding man across from him. Did he truly hate the Superintendent? He didn't know. Maybe hate was just an Old Age word, an expensive sentiment reserved for a world and a time that could afford it. The Superintendent was not just a voice, but a real person, vulnerable, on the verge of death, and regardless of which side Myron fell, whether monster or hero, Myron couldn't just let him die.

As soon as the elevator cracked daylight, another explosion sounded from the Gorge. The elevator ground to a stop with a violent jerk just as it reached the top. Steam hissed. The mechanisms emitted an unnerving slow creak. Myron rolled the Superintendent out, and following a high-pitched twang, the cable snapped, and the elevator plummeted down into the R1 Facility for the last time, permanently sealing the only other way out of Jonesbridge.

Myron tugged the Superintendent by his belt, up out of the quarry, leaving a thin trail of blood. When he reached the top, he spotted four ghosts on patrol, racing toward him.

The head ghost pulled his gun, aiming it at Myron. "Step away. Slowly, hands in the air."

Myron followed instructions, now worried they suspected him of shooting the superintendent. "I witnessed the salvage admin kidnap him—and shoot him. I saved him—from the water," Myron said.

"What water?" The head ghost looked around with a shrug. "I don't see any water."

Myron tugged at his wet smock and pointed to the entrance at the bottom of the quarry.

"Don't move." The ghost took two steps forward with the gun trained on Myron's head.

The other ghosts gathered around the Superintendent, checking for signs of life.

"Very faint pulse. I don't know if he'll make it."

"Myron Daw," the ghost captain proclaimed, tying Myron's hands behind his back. "You are guilty of bombing the munitions factory, halting the production of shells in concert with an E'ster invasion. In so doing, you are guilty of the murders of two hundred productive slogs assigned to munitions and the attempted kidnap and murder of the Superintendent of Industry."

"No." Myron yanked at the restraints. "It was the salvage administrator."

"Any one of these offenses would result in your summary execution."

"It was the salvage administrator. He did all those things.

Not me. I saved the Superintendent. He would've died down there." Looking them in the eyes, seeing the empty rage, he sighed and cast his eyes on the ground.

"Lies only breed lies."

"Customarily I'd execute you on the spot," the ghost captain said. "But we have orders. There's a bigger plan for the traitor. A rally." He kicked Myron's legs apart. "A public execution. In front of all of Jonesbridge."

"Finally some entertainment," one of the others said.

Two of the ghosts fashioned a litter for the Superintendent and began the trip back to Jonesbridge. The other two knotted Myron's feet to one end of a log and his hands to the other and hoisted him to dangle between them, his back bowed, swaying between the two ghosts as they marched back to Jonesbridge with their trophy.

Myron gritted his teeth, working his wrists back and forth for relief as they bore his dead weight on a log that obstructed his view of the sky. His head hung free, bouncing as they went. He glanced beside him to the Superintendent.

Myron had grown up sheltered, in hiding on his grandfather's farm, ducking into the potato bin or the barn when things got dicey. He had learned fear at a very young age. Quickening heart, a tingle in his chest, the sensation of falling; it was as familiar to him as the taste of mashed protein and chaff. Sorrow, that was a numbness on his head, tears, and a hollow, worthless feeling like carrying a heavy crate that turned out to be empty. Sorrow and fear were two emotional neighbors that Myron knew well. He experienced them both on a daily basis in Jonesbridge, sorrowful that he remained, sorrowful for what he saw, how he was treated, and fearful of what would come, fearful of the sorrow. The tense muscles, the stinging bile that rose up his throat when he saw his mother's lifeless body under the blanket, and the sounds of Sindra's tears when the ghosts violated her, he recognized that as anger—which always led to sorrow.

His grandfather had taught him not to hate, and only now did Myron understand that hate was not so much an extreme dislike of something, such as his aversion to mashed protein and chaff, rather it was the fermentation of his sorrow, its strengthening and souring into something repulsive. Hate, he'd only come to understand once he finally experienced love, the ugly mirror image of the beautiful fullness he'd felt when he and Sindra planned their escape in the shadows of the chapel during the best moments of his life. As he relived Coyote Man sailing away with Sindra and then imagined his own public execution, the sneering and hissing, the snapping of his neck before a throng of his fellow slogs, after all that he'd sacrificed and endured, the only thing he truly hated was his sorrow and fear. And today, he had overcome them both.

"Execute me if it'll make you feel better, but the man you want is already dead."

"Shut up, traitor." The ghost kicked Myron in the back.

The bombing had grown quiet. The explosions had ceased, and based on bits of conversation he heard as they paraded him down the main thoroughfare of Jonesbridge, the E'ster catapults, along with much of their attack force, had plummeted into the Gorge, which explained all the explosions in the R1 Facility. The ghosts marched Myron past the still-smoldering munitions plant, all the way to the administration building where the gargoyles judged him with their cold eyes. In the middle of the parade ground adjacent to the main building, on a platform ten feet off the ground, they yoked Myron into a pillory and chained his legs to the base. There he watched, over the next few hours, the gallows he would hang from taking shape before his eyes, built by the hands of workers from his shift in the salvage factory. Some sneered. A few of them spat or threw hard objects at him. Saul jabbed him with a stick.

Myron spent the night hunched over in the pillory, rebuilding in his mind the postcard and the dream of Bora Bora. He couldn't be certain what he saw in the R1 Facility, whether he truly was more adaptable, whether the Old Age scientists really did experiment on his ancestors in Richterville, but he took it for the truth. Most of what they endured here would have killed an ordinary person, so he clung to a silly hope that his neck might not break when the gallows platform gave way.

The next morning, following the shift siren and the rising of the sun, all of Jonesbridge gathered in platoons on the parade grounds. The entire complex halting production just to watch him die. A squad of ghosts clad in formal parade attire, something Myron hadn't yet seen in his time in Jonesbridge, approached the stocks.

"It's time," the ghost captain pronounced. With Myron's feet and hands in chains, they released him from the pillory.

The journey from the stockade to the gallows began, and as the hangman's noose came into focus, Myron wore the inevitability of his fate as a matter of honor. The death of a slog was unceremonious, without mourners or fanfare, no bugles, no speeches, no tears. Some claimed that even the Great Above turned an indifferent eye to the demise of a slog, their bodies heaped into a bury hole, one atop the other, until the hole filled. But today, all of Jonesbridge had gathered to watch Myron, a lowly slog, expire to the bugle call of requiem, and, as those who'd swung from the gallows before him, he would be remembered, a slog among slogs.

The procession stopped at the base of the gallows that smelled of shin pine resin. His escorts peeled away for Myron to make the last leg of the march to the executioner alone. The six stairs that stood between Myron and his final breath stretched all the way to the heavens. He stepped onto the bottom stair. It creaked, as they all did until he stood at eye-level with his executioner.

At the top, he stood before a ghost captain who slipped the noose around Myron's neck, a scratchy braid of twine, already uncomfortable resting on his collar bones. He studied the outline of the trap door beneath his feet, the faces of the slogs in the crowd, and broadened his shoulders, stuck his chin out and raised his head.

"Myron Daw," the ghost captain shouted. "For repeated duty shirking. For the destruction of the Munitions Facility Number-Two, and for being a traitor to the Alliance, I hereby sentence you to death." The ghost reached for the platform release handle.

Myron clinched his jaw, awaiting the click and the squeak of the platform hinge. He closed his eyes and searched his memory of the postcard image of Bora Bora and Sindra's face.

"Wait!"

Myron eased one eye open. An administration courier ran up the passageway, holding up his hand. The ghost captain took his grip off of the release lever.

Out of breath, the messenger jogged up the stairs and whispered in the captain's ear, after which the captain removed the noose from Myron's neck and gave him a shove in the back toward the stairs. Myron stumbled through the gauntlet of murmuring slogs.

The ghost platoon led Myron, still in chains, into the administration building to stand before the clerk where she spoke to an unseen person in the shadows and adjusted her spectacles.

"Myron Daw. Against the odds, the Superintendent of Industry has survived his ordeal." She nodded and a ghost removed the chains. "Step forward."

Myron took two steps toward her station.

"All the way." She motioned him with her hand.

"The Superintendent of Industry has implicated Cyril, the former salvage factory administrator, as the traitor." She double checked her papers. "Even though you are only a slog, given your acts of patriotism, and given the leadership opening in salvage, he has promoted you to the position of Salvage Factory Administrator effective immediately."

•   •   •

At 7:00 A.M. the following morning, the factory siren wailed from atop a stanchion in the salvage yard, emitting its familiar howl before it hiccupped and ebbed into a moan. The day shift began with no attack warning, as if the E'sters had never tried to assail the Gorge. All one hundred workers, including the foreman, Saul, stood in place on the salvage factory floor, at attention, arms straight down, chest out, eyes focused on the flag that hung like a tapestry on the towering south wall.

Myron, using the side door and bypassing entrance

procedures for the first time, walked up the staircase to the administrator's office and took his place on the factory overlook as the anthem began. His faceless shadow loomed over the south bank of workbenches the way all administrator's shadows did, but as much as he'd wished to have a larger domicile and a better job, he never imagined it would ever happen, that he would be the first and only slog to ever rise to the rank of administrator in Jonesbridge.

Following a customary minute of silence, the Superintendent of Industry began his admonition for the shift. "The E'sters have retreated." A thunderous applause sounded, audible not just from their factory, but the surrounding factories as well. "We fought well. We continued production. We lived to fight another day. And we will, because they will certainly return. And when they do, we must be ready."

Myron wondered where his airship had taken Sindra, if it had sailed her all the way to Bora Bora, and what she would think of his new position. He believed he truly loved her in every way a man could love a woman, and though he doubted he would ever see her again, he had given her the best gift he could imagine: liberation from Jonesbridge, freedom to fly.

When Myron's grandfather first tried to teach him how to fly a kite, Myron had let go of the dowel by mistake and chased the string across a ravine and up a hill until the kite vanished over the top of the next hill. His grandfather had told him that there was nothing like losing a kite to teach you how to fly one, that it was nothing but a few sticks and some old newsprint, maybe some glue. A kite lost, yes, but he had certainly hoped that wouldn't be the one and only kite

Myron ever built. As he surveyed the factory floor, Myron began a mental design of a new airship, one he could build from better parts that only an administrator could procure.

END